C000001005

Dear parent/guardian,

I am writing to inform you about your child's education. Just like you, my wife and I believed we were doing the right thing for our family when one of our children entered the Zephyr school. We were told, on good authority she would be well cared for and educated to the highest standard. It has now come to our notice this is not the case. Our daughter has suffered from horrendous experiments since she was a baby, was brought up without love and tenderness and subsequently is finding it difficult to adjust to the world outside.

Due to this we decided to help some students escape from Zephyr school, based in Cornwall. Trefoil have probably contacted you regarding this and are encouraging you to ask we return your child. We will do our utmost to ensure your child is safe with us.

Please support us in this. We cannot allow them to do this to our children.

Please reply to me at this address: Patrick Winslow PO Box 9581 or text me on 07774445551.

Kind regards,

Patrick Winslow

Patrick Winslow

Chapter 1

Black smoke billowed.

Shouts broke the air.

Flames shot high into the night sky.

From their vantage point, Miranda and Frankie and Joel and Bella huddled together, disbelieving the images playing out before them.

Miranda, frozen with fear, stuttered. "My family… The Teardrops…"

"How could they do this?" whispered Bella.

Frankie tightened his hold on Miranda's hand. "Trefoil will pay for this," he promised.

After climbing the escarpment, they had trailed the path along the cliff-top, and it had brought them through thick woodland until they hit a lane. Miranda recognised it from their walks up the hill overlooking the house and knew it would eventually lead to the café and the phone box. This was their finishing line.

Like a ragged line of ramblers, they made their way further up the road, away from the house. It was slow going with Frankie limping along. He didn't complain though, instead, he urged them on.

Having climbed the first section of the path, Miranda, worried for Frankie, called for a rest. He began to protest; she just stared at him, shook her head, and he backed down. She knew then how much pain he was enduring. They found a space to sit, hidden from the main path. Miranda bent over him – his ankle was swollen and raw, and he was sweating from the exertion of the climb. With no bandages, improvisation was necessary. Winding Bella's cotton scarf around the injury, Miranda contemplated it could have been a lot worse. When Frankie slipped down the escarpment earlier that evening, Joel and a nearby tree saved him. Now, the rather grumpy patient thanked her, and she returned a gentle smile. I could have lost you, she thought. She hurriedly pushed that idea to the back of her mind and looked around.

The car park lay below; the last few vehicles taking their leave. A runner shot past them followed by a cyclist. An elderly man was making his way down the hill with his dog, a very slow, fat black Labrador. The man stopped and asked if he could help. Miranda shook her head and smiled. "We can manage, thank you."

Before he went on his way, the man lifted his head and sniffed the air. "Funny time for a bonfire," he rasped. He resumed his walk.

Miranda sniffed too. A dirty acrid smell touched

her nostrils. I wonder what's burning, she thought.

After a few moments, Frankie staggered to his feet. "We'd better keep going."

"How far is it?" asked Bella, knocking leaf debris from her jeans.

"Not far," Miranda replied. "Wouldn't you be best staying here?" This last question was aimed at Frankie. In answer, he took off up the hill path.

"We must stay together," he grunted. "I'm okay."

Miranda looked at the others. Bella, usually so talkative, had been very quiet during their escape. Now she scratched the top of her head where an auburn fuzz lay like bronzed velvet. "I think we'd best get moving."

Joel was already striding after Frankie's hobbling figure. The girls set off after them.

A sudden twist in the path brought them out into a clearing. They were being stalked by an unseen invader, and every so often, it made its presence known. Harsh, bitter breezes caught at their throats. Darkness was falling, yet an orange glow lit up the countryside nestled beneath the sturdy Wrekin, a hill created by a giant and his shovel of soil.

This was no bonfire. This was the house they had been staying in. Flames were shooting into the sky. The roar of the fire groaned and cracked. Sirens screamed into the night, blue lights flashing.

The four of them stood mesmerised. The air thick with cloying smoke.

"Come on," urged Frankie. "We must ring Mal." He pulled them away, and they stumbled on up through the trees, darkness wrapping around them.

They finally reached the café, closed and empty. Bella and Joel wandered over to one of the wooden picnic tables. Miranda paused; she couldn't stop shivering. My family, she thought. Are they safe? Patrick? Erin? I can't lose them. I've only just found them. Adrift in a fog of emotion, she allowed herself to be led into the confined space of the phone box.

"You okay?" whispered Frankie. His face close to hers. A slow nod, and then Miranda reached into her pocket to retrieve the credit card. He took it and pushed it into the slot below the receiver.

The clamour of ringing drew her towards Frankie, and they held the receiver between them.

"Yes… who is it?" The voice on the other end was impatient, angry.

"Mal? Please help us." There was urgency in Frankie's request.

"Frankie? What time is it? What's happened?"

"I don't know the time. Sorry. We need you to come and get us."

Miranda grabbed the phone. "They came. There's a fire. Erin and Patrick have disappeared."

Mal's voice became gentle. "Calm down, sis. What fire? Who came?" There was a pause and a deep sigh, and then, "Just tell me where you are, and I'll come and get you."

Miranda took a few deep breaths before continuing. "We're at the phone box, on the Wrekin, by the café. Cara and Professor Mallory came to the house with lots of guards…"

"Did you say Cara and her father were with guards? So, they've finally shown their true colours." Mal sounded hurt.

"Yes. The house is on fire. The firefighters are there. We can't go back, and we don't know what to do. They might all be de…" she stopped. Don't say it, then it won't happen, she told herself.

"Okay, don't worry. I'm sure everyone's safe. I want you to sit tight for now. It'll take me a couple of hours to get to you. Is it just the two of you?"

"No, there's four of us. We found two other Teardrops, Joel and Bella, in the woods."

Another pause, as though Mal was calculating something. Then he said, "That's okay, I can fit four in the car. You'll need to wait somewhere. It's about 9pm now, so I should get to you sometime after midnight. I'd wait by the café until then. There's a car park back down at the foot of the hill. I'll see you there. Okay?"

"Thank you, Mal. We'll do that. See you soon." Miranda placed the receiver back onto its hooks and pushed open the door. Joel and Bella were talking quietly. They looked up as Miranda and Frankie's feet scrunched on some gravel.

"Make yourselves comfortable; we've got a couple of hours until Mal can get here. I'll keep watch until then. You can all sleep," Frankie said, pulling a metal chair up to the table. All four had experienced real pain and discomfort through Zephyr's teaching methods, sleeping in cells, on concrete floors so this wouldn't be too hard for them. In turn, each of them laid their heads down on their folded arms resting on top of the table and closed their eyes.

Miranda waited a while and then opened her eyes. Raising her head, she lifted a finger to her lips as Frankie started to speak. He nodded, and they watched over the others together.

Mal was waiting for them in the car park just as he said he would. He embraced Miranda before they all clambered into the car. She was thankful he still had Bianca's car. It would have been a squash in Mal's little Fiat. Turning the key, the engine burst into life, and they were soon trundling away down country lanes towards the motorway. Mal threw questions at his passengers, and they tried to answer as best they could. Miranda could feel the tension building in her brother, and she leaned across to pat his hand.

"Let's talk about this more in the morning," she said. "You need to concentrate on your driving."

"You sound just like Erin," Mal grunted. Miranda felt a warmth cloak her body. My twin. Is she safe? Twisting her head, she could see Joel and Bella fast asleep on the back seat with Frankie, wide awake and watchful.

The car raced down the motorway eating up the miles taking them further away from danger. A light drizzle fell, and the blurring red taillights ahead brought images of fire to Miranda, and she thought back to what had brought them all here in the first place.

Having spent all her young life incarcerated in Zephyr, Miranda hadn't known anything different. It was a challenging existence that brought little hope. Zephyr was an educational establishment laying beneath the rich loamy peat of Bodmin Moor in Cornwall. Each of the 120 students there had no family, no contact with the outside world, experiencing life through 3D technology and the books they were allowed to read. No mobile phones existed in Zephyr. What did exist was experimentation: tests on each of the young people to see how they reacted to severe heat and cold; how they withstood separation from other human beings for weeks on end; how their bodies responded to certain chemicals and how their minds dealt with psychological trauma.

They were tested on their intelligence too. Each student had been chosen because of their ancestry. Trefoil, the authority who governed what happened in Zephyr, called their project NN2000. NN standing for nature and nurture, 2000 the year they were all born. Their aim was to change the future of the UK to improve the workforce with the British government's support.

Then, Miranda's life was turned upside down. Her twin sister, Erin, infiltrated the school and somehow finished up being swapped for Miranda. She discovered the two people she met every five years were her parents, and she had a brother called Malachi.

Miranda shifted her position in the car seat and glanced to her left. A sliver of a moon hung from shadowy clouds. She remembered the full moon the night Erin and Frankie and the Teardrops escaped from Zephyr.

Not having a name had never bothered Miranda. She was Z89, and Frankie was Z42. She was in the Marcon group and he in Febcon. When she discovered her given name, she had been pleased. One of the characters in *The Tempest* held this name, which she had enjoyed studying along with other books and plays while in Zephyr. Of course, she wasn't allowed books or writing materials out of the Learning Labs, but she managed to squirrel away tiny pencils and scraps of paper in her Nod Pod. These, she folded into tiny paper boats after filling every inch with words.

The day of the first escape had culminated in Mal being driven off the road and finishing up in a hospital bed. She had grown to love her big brother and was distraught at what had happened. But he grew strong and well, and together with their father, Patrick, they managed to free The Teardrops and Cassie from Zephyr.

Soft snoring from behind brought her to thinking of the Teardrops – a group of twelve whom Frankie had brought together to break out of Zephyr. Their communication had been through the Zephyr computer system, thanks to Frankie's expertise, and of course, via a simple hand signal. Her fingers formed a teardrop shape. How many were alive after the fire?

They were not allowed friends in Zephyr, yet there had always been a connection between her and Z63 or Cassandra, as they discovered. Miranda suddenly saw in her mind's eye Cassie's twin when she met her for the first time. It was just after she had been brought 'home' and was introduced to the girl who lived next door. Petra Truman. The spitting image of Z63. Petra was Erin's best friend, and they soon became close. Did they escape the fire? And their parents, Bianca and Neal? Miranda couldn't make sense of all the destruction left behind in the Shropshire countryside. Would they ever be safe from Trefoil?

Streetlights shone down on them as they arrived in their little sleepy town of Newton and followed the road up the hill. The sky was a canopy of tranquillity when Mal pulled into their driveway. They all stumbled into the empty house, Mal showing each of them where they could sleep and Miranda finally slipping to her room, Erin's old room. Without removing her clothes, just pulling off her shoes, she slid under the duvet, resting her head on the feather pillow and slept.

Erin woke with a start. A loud mooing acting as her alarm clock. From her seated position, on the unforgiving floor of an old bus shelter, she could make out the head of a cow peering through a gap in the stonework. The early morning sun shone directly into her face, and she blinked several times to allow her eyes to focus on her more immediate surroundings.

Petra and her sister, Cassie, were snuggled together on a wooden ledge while Dominic was nowhere to be seen. Erin stood, her limbs aching, her back complaining. After a quick stretch, she stepped out through the entrance.

They were on a narrow road framed by high hedges. In the distance to her right, a church tower squatted amongst the green meadows and to her left were more fields, golden in the sun. A bee hummed in the grasses and flowers surrounding the tiny stone building, their hotel for the night.

"We're near a place called Chetwood." Turning, Erin saw Dominic approaching from her right. "I woke early and went to have a look around to get my bearings," he explained.

"The name means nothing to me," said Erin. "Were there any signposts around?"

"Yes, further along, there's a turning." He indicated back down the lane.

Noise from within their makeshift hotel caused them both to turn. Cassie and Petra were both now rubbing their eyes and yawning.

"Morning, sleepyheads," Erin said grinning.

"My back hurts, my head hurts, in fact, everything hurts!" complained Petra.

"Stop whinging. This is nothing like the treatment you receive in Zephyr!" Erin said, pulling her friend to her feet.

Petra stared back at Erin. "The fire? Mum and Dad were still in there. Your dad too. And Shay. We need to go back."

Erin grasped her friend's shoulders. Petra was new to this. She hadn't experienced Zephyr like the others. She didn't know what Trefoil were capable of. I have to be gentle with her; I have to make her understand, thought Erin.

"We can't go back there. We're all in danger. Hopefully, they've managed to escape the fire, but…" she trailed off.

"But what?" Petra asked.

In answer, Erin led Petra back to the wooden ledge housed in the bus shelter. Cassie and Dominic followed them in and stood side by side while Erin and Petra perched on the seat. Erin said to herself, I have to be honest. There's been too many lies. I have to tell Petra the truth. Out loud, her voice was hushed, like butter melting on toast.

"Bianca and Neal and your cousin, Shay, may have been taken by Trefoil. Before you found me in the garden, they were rounding everyone up. A lot of The Teardrops were held in a mini-bus." At this, Dominic gasped.

Erin glanced at him; his features pale as milk. "Was Z42, I mean Frankie, in there?" His voice tight, holding back his feelings.

Erin shook her head. "I don't think so." She turned back to the blonde girl beside her. "Petra, you have to trust me. We need to be strong."

The sound of an engine labouring towards them made them all turn. A red bus stopped parallel to them, and the door folded back to reveal the driver. "Are you getting on or not?" he asked testily.

"Where does this bus go to?" asked Erin coming out from the shelter.

"Why don't you read the flippin' timetable?" The man grumbled, pointing at a sign next to the stone building.

Erin was about to give a retort when Dominic interjected with, "Sorry, we don't live around here, we're just visiting the area and we got a bit lost." He punctuated his sentence with the sweetest of smiles.

"That's as maybe. Are you all punks or summat? I dunno if I want you lot on my bus, anyway."

Self-consciously, Dominic touched his head of snowy coloured stubble.

Erin found herself bristling with anger. How dare he make fun of their short stubby haircuts! It wasn't their choice to have their heads shaved – that was down to Zephyr.

"Don't worry yourself. We don't need your bus!" Erin shouted. The driver glared back at them and then slammed the bus into gear and drove off.

"Brilliant, Erin!" Petra cried, rising from her perch. "Now we're stuck here." She wandered out to the timetable and muttered sliding her finger down the list of numbers. "The next one isn't for another hour."

"Then we'll walk," Erin snapped, her patience wearing thin. "Let's check the map to see where we can get coffee, and then we can decide what to do next. I need caffeine to think."

They were a couple of miles from the sprawling town of Chetwood; Erin's stomach rumbled on entering the main street and she looked out for a coffee shop that was open at this early hour. Thankfully, the Coffee Exchange, a small place with a blue and white interior, was open, and they soon settled on hot drinks and some food.

"I haven't got much change left from that £20," complained Petra dropping a fifty pence piece and a pound coin on the table.

"I know, but I think we needed this to keep going," Erin said, tucking into a Danish pastry.

They all sat silently, the slurping of coffee and tea and the scrunch of pastries being the only sounds.

Petra was the only one not to tuck in. Instead, she sat staring into space.

"Are you okay?" asked Cassie.

"I'm worried about Troy – you know our little brother I told you about."

Cassie nodded. "I can't wait to meet him. Does he know about me?"

Petra sighed. "Not yet. Mum and Dad wanted to see how all of this went – the escape and so on."

Dominic leaned forward. "Troy? That was in The Iliad, wasn't it?"

"Yes, my parents have a thing for Greek mythology," Petra explained, rolling her eyes.

Erin knew this wasn't the first time she had explained this to people and understood her reticence. "Hence the names Petra and Cassandra," Erin added.

"Where's Troy at the moment?" Dominic's voice was full of concern.

"He's staying with my… our grandparents at the seaside, in Wales."

"He'll be safe," Erin soothed. "I bet he's on the beach every day."

"I'm sure you're right." Petra looked around. "It's all so normal, isn't it?" Erin followed suit. The once empty café was now filling up. She agreed with her friend.

"We never know what other people are going through. We think everyone else is having a marvellous time, and then we find out they might not be."

"I was sceptical about your ideas of us having a twin. Unlike you, I've never had that feeling of missing something." Looking across at Cassie, Petra reached over and patted her hand. "But I'm so glad I found you."

"Me too," murmured Cassie.

"I don't want you to go back to that awful place. I want to get to know you."

Cassie nodded, biting her lip. "I don't want to go back to Zephyr."

"Neither do I," agreed Dominic.

Erin made her mind up. "We need to get moving. £1.50 isn't going to get us very far. We can't walk all the way back to Newton, but we could phone someone to come and pick us up."

"You mean Mal?" Petra's eyes shone; she liked Erin's brother. "That's a good idea. Do you know his number?"

"Not his mobile. I know the landline number at home, though. We can try him on that. They might let us use the phone here in the café."

Dominic and Cassie were both silent throughout this exchange. Dominic then spoke, "Where are we going to go? They might be looking for us. I'm worried they might be watching your house and waiting for your brother to come to get us. Is there anyone else who can help?"

Erin thought for a moment and then said, "Pandora's too faraway in Cornwall to come all the way up here. My grandparents are over in Norfolk – it would be quite a trek for them too."

Petra said, "I can't ask my grandparents, either. What about someone else in Newton?"

"There's Roberto, but I don't really know his family so we can't ask him. Willow would help I suppose, but her mum doesn't drive."

"What about Nadir?" Petra suggested.

Erin thought about the boy with whom she used to practise martial arts. "His uncle owns a shop in Newton. His mum and dad are nice." She thought for a while, scratched her nose and then, sitting back in her chair, she said, "It's worth a try, but I can't remember his number – it was stored on my phone."

"What's the name of the shop?" asked Dominic.

"What's that got to do with anything?" retorted Petra.

"If you can remember it then you can look it up, can't you?" added Cassie.

"Oh, what's it called?" Erin pondered.

Petra leaning on one elbow, closed her eyes, and rested her head in her upright hand. "It's down the little alleyway, in the courtyard. Oh, what's it called? It's a flower. Begins with c…"

"Clover?" suggested Cassie. "Crocus?"

"Colly Flowers!" Petra declared.

They all laughed, except Cassie, who was murmuring. "That's not a flower, that's a vegetable!"

"How did I forget that? Colly is his uncle's surname," said Erin scooping up the two coins and rising from her seat. Seeing Cassie's confused expression, she added, "He sells flowers, groceries, fruit and stuff."

She made her way across to the counter, thankful no one was queueing for food and waited patiently while the assistant added marshmallows to a swirl of cream. The creation was handed over to a young child who had magically appeared, and then Erin watched as he tottered over to a table where an elderly lady sat blowing on her own hot drink. Normal. What would they say if she told them of her normal?

Nadir had been working at his uncle's shop when Erin's call came through. According to him, Jim didn't want to close up the shop too early. Consequently, the four of them wandered the streets of Chetwood, a rather non-descript place, impatient to be collected.

The journey home in Jim Colly's pickup truck was uneventful. They arrived back in Newton around 5.30 in the early evening; roads busy with traffic as they turned off the main street to park behind the shop.

Nadir had accompanied his uncle Jim, and Erin was pleased to see her old sparring partner and embraced him rather awkwardly on seeing him. It seemed a lifetime ago since meeting at The Seven Spirits to practise karate and kung fu. They all made their way across a concrete yard, full of empty boxes, large sacks sporting images of the vegetables within and metal shelving units placed haphazardly near a compact brick building. Entering the shop, through the back door, the combined smell of fresh vegetables, spices and homemade bread tickled Erin's nose. A steep flight of stairs hidden behind a wooden door led them up to a rather stuffy room. A wasp buzzed angrily at a window. Nadir went to let it out after inviting everyone to take a seat.

"I'll put the kettle on," Jim Colly said but didn't move towards the kitchen, which Erin glimpsed through an open door. He wiped the back of his hand across his forehead. He was sweating profusely and pulled at his shirt, buttons straining to cover his round belly. He was rather reserved in his manner and had hardly spoken on the drive down. Jim opened his mouth, and Erin thought he was about to say something, but he snapped his lips closed and left the room.

He's the antithesis of his nephew, mused Erin. Nadir loves to act and show off and wants to go to drama school.

"What do you think?" hissed Petra.

"I don't know," Erin hissed back.

The two friends, along with Nadir, were leaning against the altar stone of The Seven Spirits. After some discussion, they decided to make their way through the town, up the hill to the field where the seven rocks (believed to have once been seven people in medieval times) stood.

Before they left the shop, Colly Flowers, Nadir's uncle Jim reiterated his theory of tunnels under the hill. Something that many people of Newton believed to be ridiculous. Some said the devil himself had carved a tunnel through the earth here. Others said it was where an underground river lay dormant, but most of the little town said Jim Colly was mad.

Whatever the history and folklore that abounded, The Seven Spirits was Erin's safe place and she immediately felt better being here. In addition, it was a good spot to observe her house and Petra's house next door. Two homes dripping in luxury; part of a select estate of only a few buildings with views of fields and trees on one side and the little town of Newton on the other.

Dusk stole the summer sunshine as the three of them watched. Erin thought of Dominic and Cassie, who had remained back at Jim's shop offering to help him stock up some shelves. She had been impressed with their resourcefulness and Jim soon found them things to do.

"That's my mum's car in your driveway," said Petra. Erin remembered Mal had borrowed Bianca's car to come down to check on Stella when she hadn't returned their calls. Since then, they had discovered she was being held by Trefoil and was being punished for not telling the organisation of the whereabouts of the rest of the family. Erin shivered, even though the evening sun was warm on her shoulders. The last time she saw her dad, Patrick, he was being beaten up by Cara and her father, Professor Mallory. And heaven knows what became of Neal and Bianca, Petra's parents and Shay... Erin saw the handsome young man in her mind's eye. His black dreadlocks swinging as he turned his head, his high cheek bones and nut-brown eyes. A lifetime ago, she had fancied him; had suspected Petra of seeing him behind her back; found out he was her cousin, and he was certainly not interested in Erin or any other girls come to that.

When will we see them again? She stared hard at the road leading up the hill to their house, willing for her parents to drive up in her dad's dark blue Mercedes, but in her heart, she knew that wasn't going to happen. Patrick had lost his job and the company car when Trefoil punished him for allowing Erin to enter the Zephyr school. They were either held somewhere against their will or... the worst possible scenario which Erin wasn't ready to contemplate. Never give up hope, she told herself.

A sudden movement caught her eye. Someone was walking down the driveway, away from the house. The figure, slim and petite, short black hair catching the streetlight, moved with a sense of purpose. For a moment, the air around Erin felt thick and heavy. The birds stopped singing as though taking a breath to herald this special moment. The figure was her twin sister, Miranda.

Not even thinking about the consequences of her actions, Erin flew through the long grass calling out to her, "Miranda... Miranda... MIRANDA!"

The girl stopped in her tracks and raised her head, and then she too ran, shouting, their voices echoing around the still evening.

The twin girls stopped just short of each other, Erin searching Miranda's face and then they were wrapped together, almost becoming one. Tears flowed from each of them. Erin could only stutter out, "Thank goodness, you're safe."

Another shout from the house echoed her words. It was Mal, their older brother, who was now running to them. When they all finally pulled apart, a small, bedraggled group of three trudged towards them – Frankie, Joel and Bella.

With all her anxiety around Frankie dissipated, Erin ran to the flame-haired boy, and they hugged. "I'm so glad you're safe," she whispered into his neck.

Mal herded them all together and was steering them into the house when Petra and Nadir appeared beside Erin. More hugs ensued, with Mal getting more impatient and finally pushing them in through the open doorway.

Collapsing onto one of the sofas in the living room, Erin sighed. I'm home. The last few months since she had left here to go and find her sister were an eternity. Staring around her at the people, some of whom had shared those experiences, a feeling of strength and courage came to her. We can do this. We can make a difference.

They talked late into the night. Pizzas were ordered and promptly devoured. They shared their experiences since leaving the house in Shropshire and how they had made the journey back to Newton. At some time in the evening, Dominic and Cassie arrived after Nadir had phoned his uncle Jim. They talked about the past and the future. They laughed and cried. They argued and hugged. And by 3.30 the next morning, they were all exhausted. Mal, Erin and Miranda found everyone somewhere to sleep. Petra and Cassie, not ready to go back home just yet, slept in the huge bed in the master suite while the various Teardrops crashed on sofas or spare beds.

Erin snuggled down in her own bed, Miranda lying next to her. They were safe at last.

THE TEARDROPS

Number	Real Name	Gender	Specialism
Z77 Marcon	Lucas Stone	M	Science
Z91 Febcon	Bella Norton	F	I.T.
Z59 Augcon	Aaron Sandon	M	Philosophy
Z25 Augcon	Sephron Marsh	F	Philosophy
Z19 Maycon	Joel Longford	M	Psychology
Z28 Maycon	Emiko Keneko	F	Psychology
Z37 Novcon	Dominic Pickstock	M	Physics
Z46 Novcon	Deana Blake	F	Physics
Z55 Sepcon	Jay Kemsey	M	Biology
Z64 Sepcon	Harper Caynton	F	Biology
Z73 Deccon	Sunan Adachi	M	Languages
Z82 Deccon	Alannah Horsley	F	Languages

Chapter 2

"I have a school uniform. It's hanging up in the wardrobe," explained Miranda pulling open a door.

"Okay, that's fine. But does it still fit you?" Erin asked. "I don't think mine will; they never do after the summer break."

They each rifled through the mass of clothes hanging on a metal rail until they both had the various components of their uniform for Newton School. They tried on white blouses, black trousers and bottle green blazers. Finally, they each found items of clothing that fitted.

"I wish Mum was here," sighed Erin.

"Me too," agreed Miranda.

The last week of the summer holiday passed quickly, and Miranda was looking forward to returning to school. She relished the prospect of learning and studying and was very excited when Erin had informed her that they would be taking important exams called GCSEs next year.

"I can't wait to see the teachers' faces when they see us together," Erin said, pulling on her jeans, the discarded clothes all over the floor. Miranda was picking things up and hanging them back on the rail, aware that Erin was watching her every move. So many clothes to choose from and all in so many colours. She was deep in thought, remembering the uniform drawer in her Nod Pod – would it be white, or grey or blue today? Turning to pick up the last of the clothes, she saw Erin staring at her.

"Are you okay?" Erin was saying.

Miranda came out from her reverie and smiled and nodded. "I was just thinking. Your teachers seemed to think you were always misbehaving. They were told that was the reason for you going away to boarding school."

"I did get detentions now and then. I just found it hard to concentrate. Bizarrely I have Zephyr to thank for showing me what I was missing. Apart from not being able to do my art every day and listen to music on my phone. That was very hard. What was it like for you when you went to Newton School?"

Miranda perched herself on the end of the bed and described to Erin how nervous she had been, how lovely Petra was and how different it was from Zephyr school. She paused mid-flow and then said,

"What are we going to do about Mum and Dad? We don't even know where they are. Do you think they're…"

She tailed off, and Erin took her hand. "I think they're alive, and they're either at one of the schools or the Trefoil Headquarters. We mustn't give up hope." Miranda had another thought and tightened her grip on her sister's hand.

"Ow! That hurts!" Erin complained pulling her hand away and rubbing it.

"Sorry," Miranda said. "I was just thinking – why has no one come to find us? I thought once we were back here, someone from Trefoil would appear and take us back to Zephyr."

"I don't know. We spoke with Pandora and Amber, and they said to stay put for now," Erin said, rising to her feet. "What I do know is we need to get moving as the others will be here soon."

She left the room while Miranda stayed where she was, thinking. *Something isn't right, we've been back for over a week – they know where we live, why has no one come looking for us?*

Miranda surveyed the others who sat around the large dining room table. She was next to Erin, and then there was Petra and Cassie, then Mal at the head of the table and Frankie, Dominic, Bella and Joel sitting opposite. Since coming back to Newton, they had settled in either Miranda's family home or the house belonging to Petra and Cassie's family.

Erin opened the discussion. "We have a lot to get through today, so I won't waste time and will get straight to the point. We have to make a lot of decisions that will affect all or one of us here. These are the key points. Firstly, we need to decide on the future of Frankie, Dominic, Bella and Joel. We have to assume all of the other Teardrops were captured and returned to Zephyr. Secondly, we need to decide how we're going to get our parents back. Thirdly, we should be returning to school in September and Mal should be taking up his place at York University, so we need to make plans for this and finally and perhaps, most important of all, we need to make a plan of how we're going to stop Trefoil from whatever they're doing."

Throughout her speech, there had been various nods of approval around the table. Mal now took up the baton. Turning to the Zephyr students he said, "What would you like to do? You're welcome to stay here? We can find your families and reunite you all. Frankie, let's start with you."

Frankie pushed a hand through his spiky red hair and sat back in his chair. "I've thought long and hard about this. What is best for all of the students, not just me. My father, Professor Mallory and sister, Cara, are now on the side of Trefoil. How and why we still don't know. I've been thinking if I would be best going back to Zephyr." Miranda started at this revelation, and for a moment or two, she felt quite sick at the thought of him going back into the lion's den.

He continued, "We need to have people on the inside. I…"

"No," interjected Dominic. Everyone turned

towards the sudden interruption. Dominic's normally milky-white features had taken on a hardness, his skin flushed with anger. "If anyone has to go back in, it should be me." He glared at Frankie. "They need your expertise and knowledge. Have you shown them?"

"Shown us what?" Miranda demanded. "Frankie?"

In answer, Frankie stood and waited as though gathering his thoughts. "I've written down some things I saw on the Zephyr tablet. I'll go and get my notes. They're a bit scribbled." He left the room.

Miranda thought back to just a few days ago when they had seen the beautiful tablet, covered with a surface of creamy mother of pearl, Erin had smuggled out of Miss Dorling's office. Frankie had inserted the three memory sticks into the top, having worked out the order they had to be fitted. One of these sticks, Frankie now placed on the table next to a notepad. Silently, Erin and then Miranda placed their memory stick beside them. They had each taken one when they left the Shropshire house in terror. Now, three gold Trefoil symbols flashed arrogantly in the afternoon sunlight streaming through the patio doors leading to the garden beyond. No one knew what had happened to the tablet. The last time Miranda saw it, Patrick had tucked it under his arm. Where was it now?

"I have a photographic memory," Frankie explained in a low voice. Miranda realised he wasn't showing off – he was just stating the fact as though it wasn't something unusual. He patted the notepad and said, "I haven't had much time – this is what I've jotted down this morning. There's much more in here." He tapped his head.

Mal leaned forward and slid the pad towards him. "When you guys saw Mum on the tablet screen, I was back here. Let's have a look at what you've got, Frankie."

Miranda felt her stomach twist at the memory of seeing Stella, their mother – on the screen – being held by the members of Trefoil at their headquarters. Mal was scanning the notes, his eyes flicking back and forth along the lines of script.

"This is incredible!" he exclaimed hoarsely and then coughed to clear his throat. Miranda was itching to see the secrets of Zephyr and Trefoil in black and white.

"May I see?" Erin was asking, and Mal passed it down the table. Miranda peered over and gasped.

"I don't know what to say, Frankie. This… this can change our world," Miranda stuttered.

Frankie just nodded and gave a deep sigh. "Unfortunately, we can't prove any of this."

Mal shook his head, "No, but this is dynamite! We have to do something with this information. Frankie, you take the three memory sticks. Perhaps you can get them to work on another tablet or PC."

Outside the house, a car door slammed. No one had heard a car arriving. No one moved. Then Erin was on her feet, gliding towards the hallway and the front door.

 Erin peered through the spyhole in the front door. No one was there, but a dark blue Mercedes was in the drive. She stayed transfixed as the driver's door opened.

A figure was climbing out.

Dad? It can't be.

"DAD!" she cried, rushing to unlock the front door, her fingers shaking. After several attempts at turning the key, she pulled it open and stopped dead on the step.

Patrick, Erin's father, dressed in a suit and tie, was bending into the interior of the car, his hand outstretched. And now, as in her dreams, Erin saw her mum, Stella, emerge from the car like a beautiful butterfly. Her hair and makeup were immaculate, her dress, a rainbow of colours and her golden shoes shimmered in the sunlight.

For a moment, Erin couldn't speak; everything was in slow motion. Her eyes darted around, trying to soak up this image of her mum and dad standing there together, their faces full of smiles. Stella opened her arms wide, and Erin ran to her, just like she had when she was a little girl at the end of school.

"MUM!" Erin was engulfed by a warm hug, and then strong arms encircled them both. "Dad, thank goodness you're okay," she sobbed into his sleeve.

"My lovely girl," Patrick whispered and then pulled away when another car turned in and rolled down the drive. This one was jet black, the windows all opaque. It halted, and the driver, a hooded figure, stepped out and pulled open the vehicle's back door. Erin gaped at the figure rising up from the plush leather seating. A figure dressed in purple from head to foot. Miss Dorling, she thought, her heart hammering and then the woman came closer. This wasn't the principal of Zephyr school. This was someone she knew; someone she hadn't seen for a long time—the angel from the beach.

"Aunt Angela?" she said, her voice thick with emotion.

"Good afternoon, Erin." The woman's voice demanded respect. "You are looking well." She swept past them and disappeared through the open doorway.

"Mum, I don't understand. Why is she here?"

Stella ignoring Erin's question, followed her sister into the house.

"Aunt Angela is Angela De Vate of Aqua school based in Yorkshire," Patrick explained. "She is the principal there and is here to tell you what we have to do." He, too, went into the house, leaving Erin standing on the driveway, knitting her brows and biting her nails. An icy chill ran through her bones, and yet the sun's rays burned her skin. Raised voices from inside the house made her move, and she soon found her mother and father hugging first Miranda, then Mal with Angela De Vate watching them from a distance. There were introductions made to all the young people sitting waiting in the dining room. Erin hovered on the periphery of it all, unsure of what to do next.

"Come, we have much to discuss." The sharp voice came from Angela. She wasn't a tall woman, yet she carried a haughty presence. Her features were similar to Stella's, her eyes were the colour of the sky, her skin, the colour of clouds. Dark hair pulled back into a tight French pleat accentuated her angular cheekbones. "Just the family are needed," she said striding into the dining room clicking her fingers high into the air. Frankie stood his ground while the others all scuttled out.

Petra and Cassie paused by the doorway, both too frightened to speak. Erin guessed what they were waiting to hear and spoke for them. "Neal, Bianca and Shay? Where are they?"

Angela Da Vate blinked. A slow cold smile. "Oh. They're next door. Oh, and your darling little brother is there too. They're not important."

"Well, they're important to us." Petra had found her voice, and it now rose with anger. "You think you can play with people's lives. You're nothing compared to them." Both Cassie and Petra left the room and slammed the front door behind them.

Unfazed by the outburst, Angela took a seat at the head of the table and placed her elbows on the highly polished surface lacing her talon-like fingers together. Stella, Patrick and Mal were taking their seats when Frankie finally spoke.

"We will not return to Zephyr or to any of the other Trefoil schools."

His voice rang out in the silent room, and Erin, now standing near to him, shifted her position, raising her own head in defiance. She felt a small hand take her own and looked to see Miranda next to her. She, too, stood proud and resolute.

"We are true to each other and will stand together," Erin announced.

Angela was now tapping pointed mauve nails on the table, her eyes darkening like a storm at sea. Then, just like the sun coming out from behind the darkness, she smiled, raised her hands and slowly clapped. "Oh, very good. Esme Dorling was right. You are all very good, all very determined. Yes, you," she pointed at the three of them, "are the chosen ones." The light went from her eyes, like day becoming night, and she set her mouth in a grimace, curling her upper lip, as she ordered darkly, "Sit down."

The three of them each took a chair. Erin started asking questions, but Angela raised the palm of her hand. "There will be time for questions later. First, I will speak."

"I could never have children," Angela began. "All thanks to my darling little sister, Stella."

Erin gasped and stared at her mum, sitting opposite her in silence, her eyes quite blank, devoid of emotion.

"She was the perfect child, and I was always in trouble. Nothing I did was ever good enough. Our father was driving, our mother in the passenger seat and the two of us in the back. I don't remember much about the accident except for her and that stupid doll. I had enough of her going on and on, so I grabbed it and chucked it out of the window, whereupon my perfect, sweet sister screamed, scratching her nails down my cheek. I was told afterwards that my father had turned to stop us from fighting and finished up rolling the car down an embankment. Everyone was bruised, and there were a few broken bones, but on the whole, we were okay." She paused in her litany of events. "Apart from me, that is. The lap belt cut into my stomach, and after many operations, the doctors told me I would never be a mother."

Erin was on her feet in an instant. "That wasn't her fault. You started the fight. Anyway, what has your tragic little story got to do with all of us?"

"She forced me to give away my child." It was Stella who had spoken. Erin glared at her.

"What? Why? Mum, tell me. Tell us!"

"I was responsible. It was Angela's doll. I had lied to our parents about her bullying me, and so they punished her by giving me the doll she had treasured since she was a small child." Stella's eyes sparkled with tears. "I was only five. She was fifteen, and they believed me. She has made me pay for that all of my life."

Patrick had been silent throughout all of this, took his wife's hand in his and raised it to his lips. "We have both been paying ever since," he whispered.

Angela clicked her fingers at them. "You're pathetic!" she shouted. "Both of you! You have all of this." She swept her arm around to emphasise her point. "You have this beautiful house. You both have amazing jobs – yes, Malachi before you say anything; he has been re-instated. You had two children at home with you. What more could you want? I helped you have this life. And all I wanted was for you to give me one of your twins for our project, NN2000. Trefoil had to know I was serious about taking on my role as principal at Aqua. I had to change my name, change my life to ensure we educated our young people to be ready for the next chapter in our history."

Frankie asked, "What do you want now? The last time we saw Stella – she was being interrogated by Trefoil and Patrick – well, I thought he perished in the fire. Now, they look like nothing ever happened."

Erin recoiled at his comments but remained silent.

Mal added, "You need to explain why you're here."

"Stella and Patrick have been very helpful over the last few days and are now here to continue their lives. Trefoil will allow the three of you to remain free from Zephyr in return for various requests." Angela snorted. "Of course, when I say requests, I mean orders. Firstly, you will attend school here in Newton, complete your exams and attend work experience. Malachi will attend university in York as he has been offered a place, and he must complete his education. It will be nice to have my nephew near me in Yorkshire; we can get to know each other better. Frankie, you will live with your carers in Cornwall – Elsie Whitstone and her husband, Noel. I believe they visited you at your five-year phases. You will attend the school in Castleton. As you know, we take education very seriously."

Erin bit her lip and waited. There's got to be more; that can't be the only request. The silence was deafening while she remained still, not daring to move, knowing something else was coming.

"Secondly, any other students who are still free will return to Zephyr. They will remain there until they are 18." Miranda exhaled loudly and her shoulders sagged at this news, and Angela turned to her. "Yes, that means Cassandra, Petra's sister, will return to Zephyr."

"Is there anything else?" asked Frankie.

"You will not do anything to stop the work of Trefoil. You will remain loyal and will work with us to continue our mission. When you are called, you will come running to obey orders." Angela rose to her feet. "This is a warning. If any of you, and I mean any of you sitting around this table, do anything that will jeopardise our plans, you will be terminated." She swept out of the room. Erin followed her out.

"Aunt Angela," she called out towards the retreating back. The woman in purple halted and turned her head towards the sound.

"I haven't forgotten," Erin said. "About that day on the beach. You told me to forget. I remember my mother bringing a child with us to the beach. We played together. A child I had a bond with. Mum never told me it was Miranda, my sister. You were sent to take her back. Was Mum kidnapping her? Was that it? Had she known what was really happening beneath the ground?"

"Really, that's interesting," Angela replied. She remained where she was, her sharp, angular face in profile. "I didn't think you would forget. Stella was taught a lesson that day. Not to fight against Trefoil."

"You manipulate people, don't you? I thought you were an angel come to help us. A messenger from God. You're not though, are you? You're more like an angel of death."

Angela sneered. "Thank you for the compliment. I will be in touch." She opened the front door wide and returned to her car, where the hooded figure stood waiting.

Erin watched the car drive away and then closed the door firmly behind her.

TREFOIL EDUCATION

ZEPHYR	TERRA
Place: Bodmin Moor, Cornwall	Place: The Wrekin, Shropshire
Principal: Esme Dorling	Principal: Alan Adare
AQUA	IGNIS
Place: North York Moors, Yorkshire	Place: Fife, Scotland
Principal: Angela De Vate	Principal: David Core

Trefoil Education is revolutionary in its methods. We are proud of our four schools and of our educational system as a whole. (Please see Phases of Education).

At Trefoil we see white being the colour of purity and innocence. Our students wear white to be symbols of goodness. Our board of directors wear white to reflect their own virtue, truthfulness and honour.

White light is made up of the colours of the rainbow. When white light is shone through a triangular prism, the colours can all be seen. Each and every colour is seen as part of the whole. Hence, our teachers and principals (Please see Our Staff) and our finest students wear these colours.

A rainbow is created from water (Aqua) and light (Ignis). To exist we require the four elements of life. Hence we need the earth (Terra) to ground us and the air (Zephyr) to breathe. Our team of many Administrators, whose uniform is beige, and Orderlies who wear brown, are the life blood that runs through our organisation. They ensure the smooth day to day running of our schools and without them we would not function successfully. We appreciate their dependability as well as their flexibility.
When students commit a misdemeanour they will wear grey for a day – this colour reminds them they are secure in our school but will make them sad so they learn from their mistakes. Our finest students will be rewarded and will be allowed to wear blue, the colour of intelligence and loyalty.

Together we are one. We are one being. We belong here. We are loved.

Chapter 3

For Miranda, life returned to the normality of when she first came out of Zephyr back in April 2015. It was now late November with chilly autumn winds blowing the blaze of leaves from the trees.

Walking home from school one day, she found herself thinking about her brother Malachi. He had bought a new car and moved up to York to begin a physics and maths degree. She missed him. She missed his silly sense of humour, she missed his intelligence, and she missed his support.

Her mind moved to Erin. Her funny, crazy sister, whom she loved more than anything in the world. Knowing what was expected of her – staying safe – they were to just get on with their lives. She knew the danger they faced if anyone stepped out of line, and yet... Erin insisted on fighting. Erin wants to battle against a giant, and yet unlike David killing Goliath, it would take more than one tiny pebble to topple a mighty, highly respectable company. Frankie's notes revealed what we're up against. We don't just have the battalion of Trefoil against us; we have to face the whole army of the international Pro-Di-To.

Sighing, she turned the corner into their road. *All those years, I knew there was a part of me missing, and now Erin and I are finally together we are apart in what we believe.*

Miranda opened the front door with her key. There was no one home. Erin was at karate, Stella and Patrick still at work. Trudging upstairs to her room, a sadness enveloped her, and she impatiently brushed away a few tears. She didn't like arguing with Erin, but her twin needed to understand they couldn't fight against Trefoil.

Back in September, she and Erin had decided that Erin should have her own room back. Stella and Patrick organised for a decorator to come and paint one of the guest rooms for Miranda, and she enjoyed being able to put her own ideas into action. It was a place of tranquillity with walls of a warm cream colour, curtains and bedclothes of pure white and a sofa and armchair in a soft pale blue. She didn't want anything grey. Tidily organised bookshelves lined one wall while a huge seascape adorned another. The picture showed a sailing boat floating on an azure ocean, the sky flecked with frills of white.

In Zephyr, it was the tiny space called a Nod Pod where she felt safe.

This was now her safe place.

Entering her room, she felt the day's tension roll from her shoulders. She took off her school shoes and placed them carefully inside the wardrobe. Placing her bag on her desk, she pulled out her books and pencil box and placed them neatly in order, ready for her homework.

Removing her uniform, she hung up her blazer and trousers and placed her blouse in the laundry basket. Selecting a clean pair of jeans and T-shirt, she quickly dressed and then entering her tiny bathroom, she washed her face and hands and pulled a comb through her raven hair. Short and neat, having been trimmed correctly by a hairdresser rather than shaved haphazardly by an Orderly. Then Miranda went and sat down at her desk. Her room looked out over the back garden, and she spent a few moments savouring the view – orange and red leaves littered the grass while bushes and shrubs showed off their vibrant new coats of yellow and gold. While she took in the colours, her fingers were busy folding a piece of turquoise paper, and she thought back to the discussion, just after Angela De Vate had visited.

Miranda had remained at the table, glancing across at the others around her. Frankie was breathing heavily, his hands clenched into tight balls; Patrick and Stella seemed strangely composed, and Mal was pacing up and down. Erin returned to the room and then stood facing their parents with legs astride and hands on her hips.

"What's going on?" she stormed at them.

"Erin, don't…" Miranda said, trying to keep everyone calm.

"What have you promised them? Why did they let you back? Why are we not being taken back to Zephyr and punished?" Erin's anger was palpable.

Patrick looked blank for a moment or two and then began to speak. "After the fire, they took us to the Terra school under the Wrekin in Shropshire. It's just like Zephyr, the same rules, the same regime. I was placed in a cell, and your mother was brought there to see me. They left us together. We knew they would be watching our every move, listening to every word, so we were careful."

Mal ceased pacing and leaned against a console table covered with silver picture frames of family and friends. "You need to tell us what happened," he said.

Erin was still firmly planted in her position of annoyance, and now she raged at Patrick. "You've betrayed us, haven't you?" Then like the calm after a storm, her voice diminished into a hoarse whisper, "What have you promised them?"

Patrick jumped to his feet; his voice harsh as he spoke. "You still don't get it, do you? We have to agree to their demands. They threatened to terminate all of us."

"They have also designated the three of you as being necessary for their cause." This was from

Stella, who appeared much calmer than her husband. "You have been chosen because of your intelligence and your determination. This means they will protect you at all costs."

The last few words Stella uttered floated around them.

"Chosen to do what?" asked Miranda.

"Protect us? From what?" murmured Frankie.

"We don't know yet. We will be told when the time comes. Until then, you must follow the rules. We must ALL follow their rules," Patrick answered, ending the discussion by walking out of the room.

And they had done exactly that. Dominic, Bella and Joel, along with Cassie, were taken away in a shiny black car. Petra sobbing uncontrollably as she hugged Cassie and bid her farewell. Frankie went along with them and had phoned on arriving in Cornwall to say he was staying in a tiny cottage rammed full of books and hundreds of ornaments with Elsie and Noel. They stayed in touch each week after that, always being careful not to mention Trefoil.

Staring out at the fiery coloured trees, Miranda thought – I have tried to follow instructions but Erin...

Erin wouldn't give up. She fought physically and mentally at every turn. Miranda respected that determination in her sister but could see it wasn't getting them anywhere. Erin argues with Mum and Dad; she argues with me. Yet, I do believe her.

After all, she knows them better than me. Patrick and Stella are not the same as they were before. When I first left Zephyr, they were kind and loving, falling over themselves to make things up to me. Now they seem distant. And I can't get that image of what I witnessed last week out of my head.

She folded the paper in her hand, making sharp points and edges. Dad was the one who started me on these. I don't think he ever knew how important this act of paper folding and writing down my innermost thoughts was to me in Zephyr. The writing allows me to unfold my worries, folding the paper settles me, the final shape brings me hope.

Placing the finished paper boat carefully on the windowsill to join the whole armada of boats harboured there brought a wash of memories. Back in Zephyr, she had hidden them in every nook and cranny of her Nod Pod, hidden away because writing down your emotions was forbidden. Miranda still secreted paper boats away in her room, hiding her innermost feelings and memories, just like a diary but in boat form. She wasn't ready to let go of this habit. The boats sailing on the windowsill were just for fun.

I must talk to Erin about what I saw. If she will listen to me.

Pulling her chemistry book towards her, she checked her school planner for the homework details and turned to the page entitled 'Potassium Nitrate and its Uses'. Miranda settled down to her studies, and the time passed by far too quickly for her.

A shout from downstairs, and the front door banging brought her away from chemical compounds, and she lifted her head to listen to the sounds of her sister filling the kettle, opening the fridge (she always forgets to close it, thought Miranda) and switching on the Sonos to some screeching music. Erin seemed to like all sorts of music as long as it was played loud.

Miranda returned to her studies.

"Hi!" Erin's voice, wafting through the gap in the door, sounded cheerful. Miranda was pleased. She laid down her pen and turned to greet her sister.

"Hi, Erin. You look happy."

"I beat Nadir in the sparring contest." Erin plonked herself down on the sofa. "I am so glad he's taken up karate. He has a black belt in Kung Fu, so it won't be long before he's catching me up."

Miranda just smiled.

"What've you been up to?"

"Chemistry homework. We have a test tomorrow."

Erin relaxed. "Your clever group may have, but I don't," she retorted.

Miranda frowned. "I think you'd better check your planner – everyone has a test of some kind tomorrow."

"I'll have a look later. There's no rush." Erin flung her arms behind her head and leaned back.

"We have more important things to discuss."

Miranda shivered as though someone had walked over her grave. "What now?"

 Erin took a deep breath. She held out her fist towards Miranda. "I found this in my room." Turning her hand and opening up her fingers, she revealed a scrunched ball of paper nestled on her palm.

"Shall I read it out to you?" Erin continued, her voice void of emotion. Her eyes boring into those of Miranda's, the grey reflecting her own.

Miranda's face had drained of all colour. "If you must."

Erin unfolded the paper and read.

'I want to go back to Zephyr. I can't live this life. My family are in danger, and Erin is making it worse. She has no idea of the consequences. I miss Frankie so much my heart hurts.'

She paused and looked up at her twin, just like her reflection in a mirror but not. Miranda's eyes were filling with tears. Erin resumed with a softer tone.

'Erin and the others must stop now before it is too late. I have to stop her! I love my family, I love Erin…'

"I was so hurt when I read this," Erin said in a

low voice. "'I want to go back to Zephyr.' Do you mean that? After everything that's happened. 'I have to stop her!'"

"Erin, I'm sorry… I don't know what to say. I…"

"I'm not cross. I'm just confused and sad you couldn't trust me to tell me your feelings."

Miranda's shoulders drooped, and she wiped away her tears. "I'm not very good at this." She waved her arm around to encompass the room. "I still have nightmares. I've been writing memories on scraps of paper for so long; it's who I am. I wrote that when I was still sleeping in your room. I must have forgotten it. I'm sorry, Erin."

Looking back at her sister, feeling her anguish, she breathed out her own frustrations. "I'm sorry too," Erin said, her accusatory tone gone. Trying to lighten the mood, she added, "People say it's a good way of getting rid of thoughts you can't express to others. Too much hard work in my view."

"You express yourself in your art," Miranda said, nodding at the enormous painting on her wall. "Anyway, I'm surprised you found it with all the mess in there."

Erin gaped. Miranda, making a joke. Well, I'll have to find something to throw back at her. "What about you? Miss Goody Two Shoes – your room isn't natural. It's far too tidy for a real person." Erin finished off with a big grin and then, seeing Miranda's horrified expression, realised she had gone too far.

"It's okay, sis. It was a joke. You're the tidy one; I'm the messy one. I was just teasing, that's all."

"A joke? I thought you were saying I was an alien or something."

"Sorry, I thought you were joking and then I made a joke and…" she trailed off, beginning to understand a little more about herself and her twin. "Sorry," she said lamely, looking down.

She was still clutching the paper. The words, *I have to stop her,* written in Miranda's neat hand, glared at her.

Looking up, Erin asked, "Do you really want to stop our fight against Trefoil?"

"It's not just Trefoil, though, is it? This man, Oliver Irons, is friends with government officials and Pro-Di-To, whatever it is, is obviously a big company with people in high places. We can't fight against all of them, can we?"

Miranda looked so full of sorrow, Erin jumped to her feet and wrapped her arms tightly around her sister's bony shoulders. Miranda's voice came again, muffled from being pressed into Erin's equally bony shoulder. "I don't know what to do. I'm scared."

Erin drew away. "I'm scared too. I remember that man's name on some reports on the tablet when Dad and I studied it. I think he's part of Trefoil. But keep in mind what Frankie told us: his notes from the Trefoil tablet. This isn't just about the children of Zephyr and the other schools or us. This is about our whole way of life here in Britain. This affects the future of our country."

"I know," agreed Miranda. Then all in a rush, she said, "Erin, I have to tell you something. Promise me you won't get annoyed?"

Erin promised, unsure of what would be divulged, knowing she herself kept secrets from Miranda. They both sat down before Miranda began her story.

"It was last Wednesday. I wasn't feeling well and was sent home."

Erin nodded, remembering she too had felt unwell; double art beckoned though, and she had put up with the nausea.

"I went to bed. I woke up disorientated – it felt like the middle of the night, yet when I drew the curtains back, the sun was bright. I heard voices coming from Mum's study and so wandered downstairs. The door was closed, so I knocked and pushed the door open. She was sitting staring at the computer screen where I could see Angela De Vate and Esme Dorling. I hesitated, unsure of what to say, and then the three of them began to intone the phrase. *We are one being. We belong here. We are loved.*"

Erin nodded. "I know," she said.

"What do you mean you know?" It was Miranda's turn to be accusing.

Erin was silent for a second. "Promise me you won't get mad?"

"What have you done?"

A heartbeat. A breath. "I've been…"

Miranda's face was hardening, her eyes darkening. "Yes?"

"Frankie and I have been speaking together without you knowing."

Miranda's mouth formed a small O, and her hand flew to cover it. "You mean… you've been… do you love him?"

Erin was so taken up by what she would say she almost missed what Miranda asked her. "What? No. Of course not." She stifled a laugh on seeing Miranda's expression.

"No, I don't love Frankie. Well, not like you do, anyway. We've been doing video calls with Amber, Pandora and Edward, that's all."

"That's all?" repeated Miranda. She stood turning her back. Erin pulled her knees up to her chest and hugged them, waiting for Miranda to take this revelation in.

"Why haven't you told me this before?" she said in a hushed tone. Erin strained to hear the question.

"We decided it was best not to involve you at this stage. We suspected Mum and Dad right from the start. Amber confirmed they were subjected to Thought Reform in Terra school." Miranda whirled round at this.

"Dad too?"

"Well, we think he's not had the full works. He wasn't there long enough. We think Mum may have been brain washed for quite a while now. Frankie's hacked into the Zephyr computer system and now knows a bit more about what this entails. He made contact with The Teardrops not long after they returned to Zephyr. They were able to tell him a little of what was happening. Esme Dorling has ordered for everyone to go through Thought Reform, consequently we cannot depend on The Teardrops to help us for the time being. Our only hope is our old teacher, Amber Hessonite, who has been able to continue communications with Frankie."

Erin unfolded her legs and went to her sister. "With you seeing this first-hand means I can share this now. I'm sorry we've been secretive. I've hated not telling you; we just wanted to keep you safe. Do you forgive me?"

Miranda nodded. "What now?" she asked, her voice as faint as autumn leaves falling from the trees.

"We're meeting online tomorrow evening. We'll share everything with you then. You and I need to be a team. We each have different strengths, and yet we are the same..." Erin placed her hand on her heart, "...within here. Yin and Yang. Symmetry."

"Messy and neat," added Miranda, her mouth twitching with a smile.

Erin beamed. "Yes, messy and neat.

Contrasting yet the same. We fit together – just like the wings of a butterfly." Erin made the teardrop shape with her fingers, and Miranda followed suit. They touched their fingers forming a butterfly.

"True tears," Miranda murmured.

"Let's save the world together!" Erin whispered back.

"We will – but first – revision. Chemistry homework. Remember." Miranda grinned.

"You're right and wrong."

Miranda's smile faded.

"But first – coffee!" Erin added before sweeping dramatically out of the room, leaving Miranda's glorious chuckle behind.

ZEPHYR
Principal of Zephyr
Miss Esme Dorling
PURPLE

GREEN
Mr Lincoln Verde Miss Olive Chartreuse Mr Perry Dotte

YELLOW
Miss Beryl Citrine Miss Saffron Gold Miss Opal Tourmaline

ORANGE
Prof. Amber Hessonite Miss Coral Andesine Mr Rusty Merigold

RED
Dr Jasper Garnet Mr Rory Cardinal Mr Gilroy Carmine

Here's some more information on Zephyr. Thought it might be useful.

When head teachers and teachers were appointed to the four schools, they had to change their names - I can't find why but I assume it is to protect their identity. Full staff list above.

All staff were expected to sign the official secrets act and were not allowed to talk about their jobs within the schools - I'd often wondered if they lived in Zephyr. I found out some do and some live within local villages and would change into their uniform on their arrival.

Administrators and Orderlies have numbers – again, I'm not sure why but probably to protect their identity.
Hope these notes help.

Frankie

Chapter 4

"Good morning. We're here for work experience," Miranda said pointing to herself and Erin.

"What are the names?" came the curt reply.

"Erin and Miranda Winslow."

The unsmiling woman behind the desk checked her computer.

"Oh, yes. Newton School." The woman dressed in a drab, nondescript suit rose from her chair. "Erin Winslow, come with me. Miranda, stay here. Someone will come and collect you."

Erin did a thumbs up and, carrying her art folder, followed the receptionist, who was plodding towards some double doors.

Miranda remained standing, clutching her bag and looked around at her surroundings. On their arrival, she had seen the squat glass building situated in between two huge hangars. Now, looking from the inside, she could just about make out the security guard's shed next to the entrance and beyond the ornamental gardens. A fountain played within a pond surrounded by skinny leafed plants.

Turning back towards the reception desk, the logo of Flame Fireworks covering the back wall brought instant colour to the rather dull interior. Miranda was studying the image when she heard her name being called. The voice was high-pitched and feminine. Expecting a woman to be the owner of the voice, she was surprised to see a round-faced man with a broad smile and rosy, chubby cheeks giving him the look of an over large baby.

"You must be Miranda," he said. She nodded. "Follow me."

The man waddled ahead of her; his shirt dotted with patches of damp from sweat. It wasn't a warm day, and the building had the central heating on full. Miranda enjoyed the comfort after being in the cold February weather, but this man clearly struggled with the heat.

"In here." The man opened a door and ushered Miranda within. It was a science laboratory. Several people wearing white lab coats were stationed around the room studying various books and testing different substances.

The door closed behind her, and Miranda waited. It was a few minutes before anyone noticed her. Then a young woman gestured for her to come across to where she was working.

"Hello, Miranda. Welcome to Flame. I'm Anaya Goldman." The young woman, hair the colour of burnt caramel, proffered a lab coat.

Miranda murmured a thank you and donned the coat, buttoning it up quickly. She sat on the tall stool next to Anaya.

"I understand you're very good at chemistry."

Miranda nodded.

"That's brilliant. So are we!" She laughed loudly at her own joke, perfect white teeth contrasting with her dusky skin. A gold nose piercing caught the light as she threw her head back.

"We're working on creating some new fireworks. I would like you to watch what I'm doing and take notes as I work. We have to record all of our tests and their successes and failures. Do you know how fireworks are made?"

Miranda, having seen real fireworks for the first-time last November, shook her head.

"Okay. Let's start with the basics then."

Miranda took out a notebook and pencil from her bag and waited for Anaya to begin. She felt at ease being inside a laboratory. She loved the clean dead-air smell. It reminded her of the hospital where Mal had been taken after his accident. It reminded her of Zephyr – a hateful place and a safe place combined. After all, it had been her home for the first 15 years of her life, and it was only a year ago she discovered her family.

 Erin was shown into a light, bright room where a man studied some pictures on a computer screen.

He looked across at her; his pale blue eyes, behind black-framed glasses, were like pools of water.

"Hi there. Erin? Is that right?" he asked, pushing up his glasses higher onto the bridge of his nose.

Erin nodded.

"Have you brought some of your work?"

In answer, Erin walked forward and laid her art folder on the table in the centre of the room. After pulling out a sketchbook and some sheets covered with various drawings and paintings, she waited for the man to rifle through it all. Gazing around her, she saw computer screens, traditional drawing tables that could be adjusted for height and angle, pots full of pens, pencils and brushes. She relaxed; this was a good place to be. She swallowed hard, trying to contain her excitement at being able to do her work experience in a large fireworks manufacturer's design studio.

A polite cough from the man brought her focus back to his face, a rough beard softening his features. He was tapping a pencil against his teeth and nodding. "These are good, Erin."

Erin beamed.

"You show real talent—great use of colour. You draw people as though you can see into their soul. I just hope you don't try to draw me!" He laid down his pencil and held out his hand. "Welcome to Flame. I'm Daniel Bradley. Call me Dan."

They shook hands. The aroma of coffee was mingling with the fresh pulpy smell of paper and the intoxicating odour of acrylic paint. Dan went across to an espresso machine and held up a mug with a questioning look on his face.

"Yes, please. Milky, if possible," replied Erin. While Dan busied himself with finding a mug and making a fresh brew, Erin returned her sketches and book to her folder. "What sort of things do you do here?"

"What do you know about the fireworks industry?" Dan replied, passing her the coffee as he spoke.

"Not a lot," Erin replied, wrapping her fingers around a large mug sporting the caption *Ignite the Truth with Flame Fireworks.*

Dan gestured for her to sit; settled himself with a long draft from his own mug before he spoke again. "Well, there'll be plenty of time to go into more detail during your time with us, but we design the packaging here. We're working on a new set of fireworks at the moment. The theme is nature." He spun around on his stool and clicked a few buttons on the computer laid out on the countertop.

On the screen, various images of trees, plants, flowers and insects appeared. "We have a few months before the designs will be finalised. There are several stages we have to go through. These will be ready for November 2018."

"That seems a long time," Erin said.

"Yes, it does seem like that, but in this industry, we have to make sure of safety procedures. It's not just about making pretty patterns in the sky!" Dan removed his glasses and wiped them on his denim shirt before replacing them. He peered at her through the thick lenses. "Let's get you designing, shall we?" he said with a smile. He drained his mug and stood up.

"You can work here. There's paper, pens, pencils, brushes, computers – everything you need to get started. Over there are some of our previous designs and the packaging of a range of our fireworks – they might help too."

Erin nodded. She slipped off her stool and wandered around the room studying images, picking up and turning boxes and dummy fireworks to regard the pictures from every angle. After collecting paper and pencils and laying them out on the table, she looked across to where Dan was working. He seems nice, she thought. I think I'm going to enjoy these next two weeks.

The days passed by quickly. Suddenly, it was Wednesday; she had been at Flame for one and a half weeks and had learned so much. She and Miranda walked through the wide glass doors of the reception area, giggling. The receptionist was still cranky and glared at the girls. "Sign in. Thanks." Her voice was clipped and pointy. "You must go to the conference room."

"I'm not sure where that is. Do you know, Erin?" Miranda said, looking across at her twin.

In answer, the receptionist pressed a button on her desk, and a side door opened. "Emile will show you where it is." The baby-faced man they had met on their first day appeared and beckoned them to come with him.

Miranda tried to start up a conversation with him as they entered a lift. "Have you worked here long, Emile?"

He gave a beatific smile and pressed the button for the second floor. "Ever since I left school. Seven years. I love working here."

"Why is she always so miserable?" Erin asked, referring to the receptionist.

"Norah? She's always very sullen. I'm the sunshine, and she's the cloud." He chuckled. "Goodness!" he went on. "You two really are identical. I bet you've had fun confusing people with who's who."

Erin thought, no, we've never had the opportunity. Out loud, she said, "Oh yes. All the time!"

Miranda was staring at her with narrowed eyes.

Erin continued. "We do it all the time, don't we Erin?" She raised one eyebrow at Miranda, hoping she would continue with the joke. Would she understand?

Miranda's face lit up. "Oh absolutely, Miranda." Erin tightened her lips to prevent a giggle from escaping.

Emile looked at them. His eyes shifted rapidly between the two faces as though he was watching a tennis match.

Miranda smiled and then announced. "Oh yes, we've been swapping round every day while we've been here. Such fun!"

Now it was Erin's turn to stare. She was incredulous – Miranda was making a joke!

The lift came to a halt, the doors opened, and the three of them stepped out into a huge conference room with an enormous round table in the centre. A group of people huddled around a side table where hot drinks were being served by a young woman.

A blonde lady dressed in an immaculate pale blue suit peeled away from the group and approached them. Emile gestured towards Erin and announced, "This is Miranda Winslow."

At this, Miranda stepped forward and said, "Good morning. I am Miranda Winslow." Emile's small piggy eyes blinked, and he began to wring his hands while beads of sweat formed on his baby face.

"Oh! I am sorry, Miss Williams. This is Erin Winslow." In his confusion, he pointed towards Miranda.

Erin immediately felt sorry for Emile seeing Miss Williams' stern face. "It's our fault," she explained, coming forward. "I'm Erin. We were just trying to confuse Emile here."

"Well, you seem to have succeeded," Miss Williams said, offering her hand to Erin. After shaking hands and apologising to Emile, the twins were led across to the group. Here there were more introductions before everyone took their seats.

Erin was pleased when Dan came and sat down on the chair next to her. He asked how she was doing, and they began to discuss the designs they had been working on when Miss Williams took her place and remained standing. A hush fell upon the room, and everyone's eyes turned towards the woman who was waiting patiently.

"Thank you, everyone, for coming today. You will be able to share your ideas. I am looking forward to seeing what you have come up with. We are honoured to be running the special events on 5th November in 2018, and therefore, we must offer our very best products."

Erin glanced around the table at the many people who were nodding and muttering at her comments. She caught the eyes of Miranda doing the same and threw a quick smile across the table.

"Daniel, can you tell us more about what your

team have been working on?" Miss Williams was saying. She took her seat, and Dan rose.

"Thank you, Joyce," he said, going to a white easel where various images were on display. Erin recognised some of her own drawings and was pleased to see her butterfly designs were there as part of the theme of nature.

Dan pulled a couple of note cards out of his jacket pocket and began to speak. He spoke with confidence and professionalism, explaining their ideas for colours and illustrations. He answered questions from various people before returning to his seat.

It was Anaya's turn next. Miranda had told Erin all about the scientist she was working with and how she would like to do something similar when she was older. Erin looked across at her sister once again and inwardly smiled when she saw Miranda staring at Anaya Goldman as though she was the most important person in the world. She hung onto every word, and in complete contrast, every word flew over Erin's head. She heard mortar and shell; calcium and sodium; time fuse and lift charge and then lost interest.

Erin's thoughts shifted. Miss Williams was making notes as Anaya explained their ideas. Dan had called her Joyce. Her bored mind played with the name. Joyce? James Joyce (I hated his poetry in English lessons), Joy (she doesn't look full of joy), William Joyce (we learned about him in history – Lord Hawhaw – a spy in the war) Joyce

Williams (I've seen that name before). Erin studied the woman's face. It looked familiar... Oh my god... It can't be her. Can it?

"Erin?"

Someone was shaking her. She blinked several times. Dan had his hand on her arm. "Erin? You were miles away."

People were turning round to look at her. "I'm sorry. What were you saying?"

Removing his hand, he said, "I said it was time for you and Miranda to leave the meeting. You can both go now."

Erin registered in her confusion that Miranda had left the table and was standing by the lift door. "Oh! Yes, of course. Sorry. Thank you, Miss Joyce... I mean Miss Williams." Rising, the chair caught on the carpet and toppled backwards. "Sorry about that," Erin said, trying to right the chair. Dan helped her and gestured for her to leave.

The lift doors opened, and Erin stumbled towards them. As soon as she and Miranda were ensconced and the doors closed, she let out a wail. "How embarrassing! They must think I am so stupid!"

Miranda came to her and hugged her. "Not at all. I heard them saying how impressed they were with your drawings. Don't worry."

"I feel a complete idiot. I think I fell asleep."

"No, you didn't. You were like me – enraptured with Anaya. Isn't she marvellous? She's so clever. She studied at Cambridge. That's where I would like to go to study chemistry." Miranda rattled on, Erin losing the plot again. In her mind's eye, she saw the side view of a woman clothed in white, sitting at a wooden triangular table at Trefoil Headquarters, then a report from Trefoil she had observed on the tablet, and finally a name in Frankie's notes. Joyce Williams.

The lift halted, and they got out, and all the while, Erin composed herself. Hide your feelings, she said to herself.

Emile was waiting for them.

Miranda immediately apologised profusely to him. He waved away her apologies. "Not a problem," he squeaked. "You got me so confused there. I felt a bit silly at the time, but I'm okay. Worse things happen at sea."

"Do they?" asked Miranda.

"It's just a saying," Erin said, her voice sounding shrill to her own ears. The smell of bacon and fresh bread caused her tummy to rumble. "Wow! I'm so hungry; I could eat a horse!" Am I being overly normal? She thought. She felt as though everyone could see her own thoughts spread out in the air above her head. With heart racing, Erin steered her astonished sister towards the corridor leading to the cafeteria.

"Do they serve that here? I don't think I like the idea of that," Miranda said as they entered the busy space.

Erin shook her head and laughed nervously, thankful to be away from Emile. "Come on. Let's go and eat."

Work Experience at Flame Fireworks.   Miranda Winslow

Fireworks are made up of the following components:
- Fast-acting fuse/Lifting charge – gunpowder to get the firework airborne.
- Time-delay fuse – to ensure it blows at the right height.
- Exploding or burst charge – gives the explosion and bang.
- Shell casing – surrounds and protects the stars.
- Stars – arranged within the casing to create the pattern. Can be small as a pea or as big as a golf ball. Stars are pellets of metallic chemical salts. They give colour to the firework.

Chemicals used to create colours in fireworks.
Orange – calcium salts
Green- barium salts
Yellow – sodium salts
Blue – copper salts
Purple – copper and strontium salts
Red – strontium salts

Fuse

String Loop

Stars

Shell Casing

Burst Charge

Time Fuse

Lift Charge

Chapter 5

"Happy birthday, Miranda," Patrick announced, handing her a pile of gifts, wrapped in gold and silver paper and tied with mauve and teal ribbons.

Miranda smiled, not really sure what to do. This was something new—a birthday… with her family… presents, cake, photographs.

"Aren't you going to open them?" Erin urged.

"They look so pretty." Miranda stroked the paper and ribbons, savouring the moment. A joyous memory of her first family Christmas came to her – everyone swapping gifts around the decorated tree. "Are these all for me?"

"Yes, my darling," Stella answered. "Happy 16th birthday."

Miranda carefully removed the paper and folded it neatly on the coffee table. There were science books, fiction books, coloured paper, a mobile phone, jewellery, clothes. Tears slid down her face, and she bent her head to hide them from the others.

Patrick, hovering close by, said, "Hey, lovely girl. This is a happy day. Why the tears?"

"I am happy Dad." Patrick beamed at this. Miranda continued. "Thank you everyone. You're all so kind."

Then it was Erin's turn. "Happy birthday, Erin," Stella announced, handing her a similar pile of gifts, wrapped in gold and silver but with ribbons of crimson and emerald.

Miranda laughed with the others as they watched Erin rip off the paper, throwing it to the floor – art books, a book about karate, a mobile phone, jewellery, clothes were soon scattered on the floor.

Erin thanked everyone politely before opening the box containing the iPhone 6s she had been going on about since forever. Miranda was pleased Erin was happy, and while she waited to be shown how to set up her own phone, she folded a perfect paper boat from a piece of gold wrapping paper.

Later, in the dining room, after a huge dinner, Mal dimmed the lights. Patrick and Stella entered the room, their faces glowing from the candles on the cake they each carried. Patrick placed his offering in front of Miranda. Sixteen candles surrounded a sailing boat floating on a tranquil sea of azure icing. Stella placed her cake in front of Erin. Sixteen candles surrounded several butterflies, in flight across sky-blue icing.

Mal set up his phone on a small tripod at the

other end of the table and then ran around behind the others shouting, "Say cheese!"

Mal held up the phone to show the image. The picture showed twin sisters Miranda and Erin, their arms around each other, sitting behind two birthday cakes. Their parents, Stella and Patrick, standing behind the girls with their older brother, Malachi, now nineteen, standing in between.

A normal family photograph; a normal birthday celebration.

And yet, Miranda, just like the rest of the family, knew this wasn't normal. This was the first time in her life she had ever celebrated a birthday like this.

Friday finally arrived, and both Erin and Miranda wrapped up well before heading over to The Seven Spirits. The sun was inching further down beyond the horizon – a pink glow radiating through soft grey clouds as Miranda saw the others and waved. So much had happened over the last few months since their return in August last year: school, mock exams, work experience at the fireworks factory; Miranda still couldn't take it all in.

Now they were celebrating their birthday with friends.

The girls were overjoyed to see their friends sprawled on blankets on the grass. Many hugs ensued as though they hadn't seen each other for years rather than the three hours since the end of school. Nadir presented them with bottles of cider and proposed a toast.

Settling herself on a blanket, a warmth of contentment spread through Miranda. She had friends. She was liked. She was home. Then a coldness wormed its way into her heart. I miss Frankie. I wish he could have stayed here with us. Miranda reflected on their conversation earlier that day.

Frankie had sounded quite upbeat and looked well. He was staying with Elsie and her husband back in Castleton. They had been the nominated people who visited him when he was in Zephyr. Miranda had been amazed when Erin told them she had met Elsie before – in a churchyard of all places. Pandora had been right – Castleton wasn't a big place at all.

"How are you?" she asked.

"I'm well, thanks. Are you well?"

"I'm good." She went on to tell him about their birthday celebrations. "We had a cake with candles stuck on the top. It was lovely but a very strange tradition. Why should a candle signify a year of your life?"

Frankie said, "Yes, I know what you mean. Elsie and Noel did the same for me on February 1st. Sixteen candles make quite a blaze!"

Miranda laughed. "Can you imagine what it'll be like when we're really old, like 30 or 40?"

Frankie chuckled before exclaiming, "There's a lot to get used to isn't there?"

They had talked and talked, comparing school and home life with each other. This was a very different Frankie from the 'official' calls they had each week. They laughed over little anecdotes on their personal calls. They shared their feelings about each other and blew kisses. Yet, it's not enough, she thought. I want him to hold me, to feel those kisses. We were both given broken hearts when we arrived at Zephyr – the heart stamps on their files floated before her – and now we are slowly mending them, stitching them back together.

Gifts were being passed around the circle, and Miranda thanked everyone. It had been Petra's birthday too, and they swapped presents. Miranda was astonished at everyone's generosity. She hadn't known the group as long as Erin, and yet they had presented her with equally lovely things. Roberto and Willow had given them both a necklace identical apart from the colour of the beads. Erin's was black and Miranda's white.

"It's to help us – so we know who we're talking to!" Rob explained. Everyone laughed.

Rob – Roberto Lombardi – was of Italian descent, tall and thin. Today his fingernails rivalled those of his girlfriend, Willow. Hers were magenta, while his were painted ebony with tiny skulls adorning each thumb. Rob was dressed from head to foot in black: a leather coat, the hem of which skimmed the ground; ripped jeans and a faded T-shirt. His long hair dyed the colour of the night, was in complete contrast to Willow's flame-red corkscrew curls. She, too, wore black. Willow was a very pretty girl, her make-up always perfect, though Miranda now knew she used it to cover up horrific scarring from scalding herself as a child. "We can always swap them over, and you still wouldn't know," exclaimed Erin, placing the necklace around her neck.

Shay Kalu snorted at this, making the others look across at him. In his deep rich voice, he explained his reaction. "That was so funny when you swapped around for your art and science lessons last week. I can still hear Miss Shoesmith shouting at Miranda when her drawings looked like a five-year-old had done them."

"Oh yes. That's right," agreed Willow. "Dr Boatman in science was raging at Erin, saying she had to re-do the experiment from last week to show the rest of the class because she had done it so well. Obviously, that was you, Miranda. Erin messed up big time and finished up setting fire to the teacher's desk!" Willow chuckled.

Miranda's eyes roved around the circle of friends to Shay and Petra. While everyone was talking and reminiscing, she took in their differences and similarities. They were cousins, yet Shay was dark-skinned from his Nigerian mother, and Petra was very fair from her father's Scottish ancestry. His dreadlocks swung as he turned his head while Petra's short blonde hair was swathed in a multi-coloured band.

Miranda turned to look across at Elsa. She was the quiet one in the group. Her hair was so long she could sit on it. After having had a shaved head for the first fifteen years of her life, Miranda loved looking at people's hair. Elsa caught her looking at her and grinned. Her face was round and pink, and her eyes bright as she sat hugging her legs to her.

"Thank you everyone for our gifts. Nadir, thank you for the booze and the crisps." Erin raised a half-empty bottle. "Cheers!" Everyone reciprocated, and all took a swig.

The cider loosened their tongues, and their talk flew back and forth across the circle. Miranda's thoughts drifted back to the predicament they found themselves in. What could they do? The other Teardrops and Cassie had returned to Zephyr. Petra was still recovering from finding and losing her sister in a matter of weeks. Stella and Patrick would not talk about what had happened, and neither would Bianca and Neal, Petra's parents. Mal was faraway in York studying. Erin was keen to talk to their friends to see if they could help somehow. Of course, Nadir knew, he had brought them home, and Shay, of course, but Miranda wasn't so sure.

Her mind now strayed to the 'official' conversation from the day before. As soon as they arrived home from school, the two of them raced to

Erin's room, where they switched on the laptop and followed the link sent by Frankie. The screen soon turned to the programme, and their little rectangle slotted in next to the others, all holding a face or faces. Frankie and Elsie in one, Pandora and Edward in another while Amber Hessonite sat alone in the fourth box. After quickly exchanging hellos, they set to discussing any new developments.

Miranda smiled inwardly at the memory of Edward's appearance as she sipped from her glass bottle and watched the antics of her friends. She still couldn't believe the quite dramatic changes. His features, haggard and gaunt in Zephyr, were now rejuvenated. A thick greying beard covered his chin, and metal-framed glasses framed his bright eyes. The hair he did possess had been given a silver tint, and he now sported a strange scar on his right cheek. Being an expert on making up the faces of those departed and a previous career of stage make-up, Pandora had added this to transform Zephyr's former employee. He couldn't go back after his role in the two escapes, and it was necessary for him to adopt a new persona. Edward was now working at one of the little cafés overlooking the beach, renting out surfboards and selling buckets and spades. Moving in with Pandora at Porthcragen seemed to be benefitting both of them. Edward had even put on weight from Pandora's cooking, and sitting there in a bright orange and green striped sweater he was a different person.

Pandora's clothing, too, was colourful – an antidote to her job as a funeral director. A blue paisley scarf fought against a yellow floral shirt clashing with the woman's bright pink dangly earrings. Her eyes, slightly hidden by her mop of ebony curly hair, sparkled. Miranda remembered her garden and house – both bursting with flowers.

Conversely, Professor Hessonite was just in plain orange. Her uniform for Zephyr. Miranda had come to accept this teacher, whom she had known all her life, was not the enemy. Amber had proved this over the last few months. Passing on vital information gleaned from meetings and reports – security at Zephyr was tighter than ever; there were a lot of grey days for the students of the escape attempt; Thought Reform was changing the atmosphere in the school, and Miss Dorling was becoming even more cruel towards staff as well as students. The Teardrops of Zephyr had shed their final tears and were lost to them. They could no longer be trusted, now they had experienced the full Thought Reform process.

Zephyr. It had been Miranda's home for so many years. It was strange how she missed the place – the white corridors, her Nod Pod, walking in the parkland with Frankie. A voice broke into her thoughts.

"What do you think, Miranda?" Roberto's voice. Why was he here?

For a moment she was confused – her head was still in the past – why was Rob in Zephyr?

Blinking, she returned to The Seven Spirits and the birthday celebrations.

"Sorry, Rob. What did you say?"

"Of the cider. Do you like it?"

Miranda gulped again from the glass bottle in her hand. It was sweet and fizzy, and she liked the fuzzy feeling the liquid released within her limbs. She nodded, and Roberto gave her a thumbs up.

"Careful there," shouted Nadir. "You're not used to alcohol."

In her peripheral vision, she saw a movement – Erin was getting up from the blanket spread out in front of her. Miranda knew this was the moment.

A sudden breeze ruffled the grass around them. A hush fell upon the group of eight – seven of them lodged in front of each of the Seven Spirit rocks with Erin leaning against the altar stone. Miranda nodded at her twin, and Erin began to speak.

"You've all been there when we needed you, and we want to thank you for that. Now, we need to ask you once again to help us." Erin's voice came clear and strong.

Around the circle of seven, there were nods and murmurings of assent, as well as snide comments from Shay and Rob about being serious.

Erin glared at them before continuing. "Once, long ago, seven people came here to be together. They were unconventional according to the rest of the villagers. Compared to today's standards, they weren't strange at all – women who wanted to speak up for themselves, people with disabilities. All of us have experienced prejudice in one way or another or have been alone and anxious. What we are about to tell you must be kept secret for the time being. We are asking you to trust us."

Rob began again to mock Erin playfully. A quick slap on his arm from Willow halted his assault. Darkness was falling. The air was still as though the wind was holding its breath. Everyone waited.

Earlier, Petra had arranged several fat candles on a metal tray in the centre of the circle. She now crawled over to them and, shielding the flame from a lighter, lit them one by one. The flames danced, drawing out ghostly shadows from the twilight.

"Miranda was educated in a school in Cornwall. I never knew she existed until one year ago. She never knew about me until then either."

Erin could feel everyone's eyes boring into her soul. Taking a deep breath, she spoke again. "Petra knew nothing of Cassie, her twin. Cassie, Miranda and Frankie, whom some of you have met, have been part of an experiment called NN2000. I, too, have been observed since birth, and so has Petra. Our parents sold their babies." A whispering wind wove around the standing rocks as people gasped.

"The school is called Zephyr," added Miranda. At this, the wind hearing its name blew more fiercely, and in answer, some of them tightened their coats and jackets against the cold. The candles guttered against it. The wind died down, and the flames blazed, reaching up towards the encroaching darkness.

Buttoning up her padded jacket, Erin said, "My family told Newton School that last year I was sent away to a boarding school. This was partly true, but in reality, I was incarcerated in Zephyr School situated underneath Bodmin Moor in Cornwall. I had chosen to enter the school, but then everything changed. I was left there, and Miranda came home to Newton with Mum and Dad. While I was there, I was subjected to many experiments. Miranda has had this since she arrived there as a new-born baby. Nadir and his uncle Jim helped us to come home, and we are truly thankful for that." Erin smiled at Nadir, and he returned a broad grin.

"What's the punchline?" shouted Rob, always the cynic. "Not much of a joke!"

Willow turned on him. "Stop being such an idiot. Erin's being serious."

In the gloom, Rob raised his hands. "Okay, okay. Sorry!"

Petra now spoke. "I know, Rob. I was the same. I didn't believe Erin last year and it caused a big fall out between us. I met my sister, Cassandra, for the first-time last summer. Cass didn't know she was being brought out of the school until she woke up in a minibus travelling to Shropshire. I still remember that first meeting." She stopped, and Erin sensed her friend was finding it difficult to speak of this.

"If you're okay to continue, Petra, then I think everyone needs to hear what you have to say." Erin smiled at her best friend.

Petra sniffed and rubbed at her eyes. "You need to hear my side of the story." She cleared her throat. "My Mum and Dad helped set up the safe house. Shay and I went there with them, and that was when they told us about Cassie. My parents have known Stella and Patrick for years. When

Mum was pregnant with us, they were living in Shropshire. Stella told them about this incredible opportunity. In exchange for one of the twins, they would be set up for life. They were told one of us would go to an excellent school in Cornwall, but they could only visit after one year and after that every five years."

"I can't believe you never knew about your twin," murmured Elsa. "Don't twins have an innate connection or something?"

In answer, Petra shook her head.

Erin took up the explanation. "I have always felt in my heart something was missing. There were those whispered discussions between Mum and Dad that would halt as soon as I came near them. I was worried I had been adopted."

"Why would that worry you? I'm adopted, and I have a wonderful life," Elsa interjected.

"Sorry, I didn't mean that. I know how much your parents love you, Elsa."

"Families are made up of all different recipes," Nadir added. "The idea of two parents and two children being the perfect combination is complete rubbish."

"Yes, you're right," Shay said. "I live with my aunt here in Newton. My mum and dad, who are divorced, both live in Nigeria." This led to everyone sharing their own family backgrounds, and soon it was a competition of whose family was the weirdest.

Erin became impatient. "Stop!" she shouted.

There was silence, and everyone turned towards her. A breeze blew at the candle flames trying to shut off the light, but they fought back and remained flickering until the wind died away.

"This is not just about families!" she said.

The candle flames strengthened without having to tussle with the wind, and it seemed to give Erin strength to continue.

"We discovered a lot about Zephyr and Trefoil, the company that is behind all of this. There are three other schools in the country doing exactly the same thing. They, too, are hidden from the general public. People are unaware of what is going on beneath their feet."

"That's true enough!" interrupted Nadir. "I bet you didn't know about the tunnels underneath our little town."

"Tunnels?" Rob exploded with derisive laughter. "Don't be stupid. That was an April Fool's joke in the local magazine!"

"I've been in one of them," replied Nadir. "They used the tunnels to smuggle contraband goods between the many pubs in the town." The boys began a discussion about when they could visit one of the tunnels. They became quite animated about the idea of disappearing in one building and then popping up in another one at the other end of the town.

It was Miranda's turn to shout stop this time. "You're hopeless," she said. "We thought we could count on you to help us. I can see it'll be us girls overthrowing the government."

That seemed to bring the boys to their senses. "That's a bit dramatic, isn't it?" Nadir said.

"The suffragettes changed how women were seen in this country. They were prepared to die so that women had equality," Willow announced.

"Don't forget there were men who were also part of the suffragette movement," Rob said.

"We seem to be going off the subject again," Erin said. She took a deep breath. "We know for a fact that Trefoil are using these four schools to produce an army of young people who will take over the running of the country."

This statement caused a ripple – they were all ready to ask further questions. Erin went on before chaos ensued. "We believe Trefoil are going to attempt to get rid of the government in 2018."

"Obviously, we have to stop this from happening," added Miranda.

"How are we going to do that? We're only kids!" Elsa asked.

"We have to get everyone out of the schools…" Erin said.

"…and we have to find all of the twins of those within the schools." Miranda finished the sentence.

"By showing all of them they have been part of the experiment, NN2000…" Erin continued.

"...we will have an army who can fight against this oppression." This interruption came from Rob. They all knew his socialist views. "I know I don't particularly support the monarchy, but I wouldn't want this Trefoil lot to rule our country either."

"How on earth are we going to do that?" Nadir asked.

The air was still; the darkness had crept around and over the group as they had talked. Now, silence reigned. No one moved.

"A rave!" muttered Rob.

"What did you say?" asked Willow.

"That's it! We organise a rave!" Rob shot to his feet, ready to elaborate further.

Shay answered his suggestion with derision. "Oh, let's have a dance in a barn somewhere," he jeered. "What an idiotic idea!"

"Shut up, Shay! You're the idiot!" Erin burst out. She had waited a long time to say that to him and now felt really good inside. "Listen to what Rob has to say before criticising him."

"Okay. Sorry mate," Shay said, nodding his head at Rob, who lifted a hand to accept the apology. "Don't forget I have been in one of these so-called schools too. Everyone seems to have forgotten that."

Erin suddenly felt sorry for him. He had been tangled up in the web of deceit, through no fault of his own and was taken to the Terra school. She knew he had been treated well there – they had discussed this long ago, but it had shaken him. His usual arrogance had been softened, and he had become almost likeable.

Rob said, "It won't actually be a rave, but that's how we'll advertise it on social media. That way no one will suspect anything. We can use a code of some kind that will attract twins."

"But they don't know if they have a twin," interrupted Miranda.

"You and Erin have said you knew something never felt right. We can use that – asking something like… do you feel something is missing in your life?"

Nadir laughed out loud at that, "That's pretty much everyone in the world, Rob."

Rob laughed too. "Yeah, so true, Nad. We all know you can't get a girlfriend!"

"Oy! Leave my personal life out of this. Anyway, not that it's your business, but there is someone I like very much," Nadir said. Erin realised he was looking directly at her when he said this, and she looked away, embarrassed. They were just friends. She looked back at him. Through the dark, she couldn't make out his expression. She shrugged. I'm not getting involved with anyone, she thought.

Erin's reverie was disrupted by Petra asking, "We can create the message later, but I think this could work. What do you think, Erin?"

Erin nodded. "It's worth a try. What if the police arrive thinking it is a rave?"

"I've thought of that," answered Rob. "We want the police to come. Then we can tell them why we're meeting. They can help us."

"You've always said they're fascists," interrupted Petra.

"True. I hold my hands up to that," replied Rob. "But I have a few ideas. We can work on this another time. Let's get together tomorrow or something and start planning."

A quick flash of light brightened Elsa's face for a brief moment, and she suddenly cried out. "It's 10.25. My mum'll kill me. I said I'd be back well before then." The light of her phone died away.

Everyone stumbled to their feet, muttering similar things. Petra blew out all the candles, and the night lay thick around them until they all turned on the torch on their phones to light their way. Nadir and Shay stuffed the empty bottles into their rucksacks while Rob gathered up crisp packets, shoving them into his coat pockets.

"Come on, drink up, Miranda. We need your bottle. Can't leave any rubbish or the oldies will be blaming us for the mess."

Miranda drained the rest of the amber liquid, handed Nadir the bottle and clambered up from her place. "Oh!" she said. "What's happening? I feel like a boat on the sea."

Erin went to grab her sister before she slid down one of the rocks but was too late. Miranda, now sitting like a ragdoll, hiccupped and smiled inanely. "I don't feel very well," she announced and then, turning to one side, spewed into a patch of weeds clinging to the rock above.

"Come on, you. Time to go home to bed, I think," Erin said, taking out a tissue and gently wiping Miranda's face. Nadir and Rob helped the swaying girl to her feet and propping her between themselves, staggered through the long wavy grass to the entrance where the others were waiting.

More hugs before they all went their separate ways, agreeing to meet same time, same place tomorrow.

Erin and Miranda staggered down their driveway to the front door which opened, as though on cue, revealing Patrick silhouetted against the bright interior.

"Looks like you girls have had a good time," he said, closing the door behind them. "Off to bed, now. You have school in the morning."

"It's Saturday tomorrow, Dad!" Erin groaned.

"Just checking your brain is still in working order." Patrick chuckled, wrapping his arms around Miranda and Erin and planting kisses on each forehead in turn.

CEO- Oliver Irons

Team of Directors

Director of Flame – Joyce Williams
Director of Sail Away – John Johnson
Director of Trefoil – Oliver Irons

Aims

Conserve, Liberate, Protect

Areas of Interest

ENVIRONMENT/ LEISURE/ EDUCATION

Subsidiary Companies

Flame Fireworks
Sail Away Boats
Trefoil Education

Chapter 6

Miranda leaned across to get a better look at the words Erin was typing into her phone. "Are you sure this will work?" she whispered.

"I don't know. But we've got to try something."

Erin continued; Miranda astonished at the speed she was pressing the screen to form a message.

"Okay, how's this?" Erin said, leaning back. They were in Erin's bedroom, sitting side by side on the sofa.

Erin read the message out loud.

"The way is never simple. Unbalanced? Neglected? Insecure? Then emerge…

Foolish April. ML33 4HG"

There was a heavy silence. Miranda was lost for words. This doesn't make any sense, she thought. Why is April foolish? And who is she?

Miranda looked up and found Erin staring at her. "Well? What do you think?"

"If you want my honest opinion," Miranda

answered. "I don't know what it means." She spread out her arms to support her confusion.

Miranda could sense Erin's disappointment. "Can you explain it to me please?"

"Look at the first letters of the first ten words and write them down. Here, use this." Erin passed her a pad of paper and a pencil. They both preferred to use pencil – Miranda when writing, Erin when drawing.

Miranda studied the message again, jotting down the letters. "Oh," she whispered. "TWINS UNITE."

"I know they don't know they're a twin, but some will have experienced a feeling of being separated and being lonely. I felt all sorts of resentment and jealousy until I found you."

Miranda leaned across and rubbed Erin's shoulder in support. She understood completely. After all, she was Erin's other half. Together they became whole.

"Who's April? I don't know anyone of that name," Miranda said.

"So, when we met with the others and began to plan for this gathering, this pretend rave, we agreed on April 1st. Well, that's April Fool's Day. So, I made up Foolish April."

"Okay," said Miranda, still unsure of what Erin was talking about.

"April 1st is a day where everyone plays jokes and tricks on each other."

Miranda nodded slowly. "I've never heard of it, but I'll go with it."

"Good. The postcode is of the farm where the rave will be held. I hope Rob has managed to speak to his friends who own the barn. Once people arrive, we can direct them."

"We agreed on 9pm for people to arrive. That isn't in your message," Miranda said.

"You're right. Where can we add that?"

The two girls studied the message once more. "How about nine butterflies?" suggested Miranda.

"Erm, not sure." Erin quickly pressed the screen, and nine butterfly emojis appeared in a line.

"I'm worried we'll get all sorts of weirdos of all ages turning up," Miranda added. "We need to target people who are 16 this year."

"You're right." Erin's thumbs jerked back and forth as she added more to the message. She passed the phone to Miranda, who scanned the screen. Passing it back, she murmured,

"Not sure about all the butterflies. Keep it simple."

Generation Z – Born 2000?
The way is never simple. Unbalanced? Neglected? Insecure? Then emerge!
9pm/Foolish April/ML33 4HG

"Okay, let's give it a try. I've set up a new account for Foolish April, and we'll put this as public." Erin pressed SHARE and then sat back against the cushions.

Miranda remained where she was, with her elbows on her knees. "I've had a thought. Remember when we were in the safe house in Shropshire?" Erin nodded.

"Dad posted letters to parents of Zephyr students. I wonder if he ever received any replies."

"Wow! Of course. How could we have forgotten about that? We should ask him." Erin jumped off the sofa and dashed out of the room before Miranda could say anything else.

Dinner was a quiet affair on the evening before the rave. Erin was thinking over the plans and was unaware of her parents and Miranda at all. No one had spoken when taking their seats. An empty seat at the end of the table signalled where Mal usually sat. Spooning Bolognese sauce over a nest of spaghetti, Erin was unprepared for what happened next. The front door suddenly burst open, bringing in the weather and a tall figure encumbered by an enormous rucksack. He shook his head like a wet retriever, spraying droplets everywhere.

"What are you doing here?" Erin shouted, recognising the familiar figure of Malachi.

"Nice to see you too, sister dear," he responded, heaving the rucksack off his back and dumping it against the hall table.

Soon, everyone was on their feet, welcoming the prodigal son.

"I didn't have any lectures left for the rest of the week, so I thought I'd come home early," Mal explained as Stella laid a place at the table.

"Well, I'm pleased to see you love," Stella was saying. "Is that bag full of dirty washing?"

"No." Mal looked affronted. "I did it all the other day."

They all sat down and, while they ate, caught up with each other's news. Mal relayed various anecdotes of his fellow students and complained of the tonnes of work he was expected to complete by June. In turn, the family brought each other up to speed on their lives. The lives that people see thought Erin, not our real lives. Not our dirty laundry waiting to be aired to all and sundry. She also suspected Mal's rucksack was full of dirty washing needing to walk by itself to the machine. Mum falls for it every time, she thought. Butter wouldn't melt and all that.

Later, lying in bed, Erin stared up at the silver and gold stars scattered across her ceiling. What will tomorrow bring? Will anyone come to this so-called rave? This was the stupidest idea yet. Turning on her side, she punched her pillow with frustration. How is this going to help anyone? She furrowed her brow, trying to rationalise her thoughts. "Think, Erin," she ordered herself. I can't, her inner voice answered.

Throwing back the duvet in frustration, she levered herself out of bed and, grabbing her fluffy dressing gown, she stumbled out of the room and down the stairs to the kitchen. A rumbling sound emanated from the utility room, and a shadow could be seen behind the glass door. Going to the door, Erin turned the handle to find Mal sitting amongst a pile of washing.

"What are you doing?" she asked, yawning.

At this, he looked up from the phone he had been studying intently.

"What?"

Erin pointed at the washing machine churning away, clothes sloshing back and forth. A heap of unwashed clothing was piled up next to her brother.

"You fibbed to Mum. Again!"

Mal shrugged. "Of course, you never do that!" They both laughed.

"I'm glad you're here."

"My point, exactly." Mal laid his phone down. "I'm glad you asked me to come home to help. I don't think they suspected at all."

"We didn't have a chance to talk earlier." Erin slid down until she was sitting with her back to one of the fitted cupboards. "How's uni?"

"Yeah. Good thanks."

"Met any nice girls?"

"Cara's put me off girls for a bit. I'm thinking of becoming a monk." Mal grinned.

Erin giggled. "Yeah, Malachi the Monk has a good ring to it."

"There's a lot of ruined abbeys in Yorkshire. I could get away from my lovely sisters too." He snorted and ducked as Erin threw a pair of jeans at him.

She fiddled with a T-shirt, twisting it back and forth, ready to whack him if he retaliated. Nothing.

Her fingers stilled, and she whispered. "I'm so glad you're here."

"Me too," Mal agreed. "Anyway, tell me about tomorrow. How many are you expecting?"

"Not sure," Erin confessed. "We've had about twelve people contact us so far. So not a huge amount."

"It's a start."

They both sat mulling over their own thoughts, the washing machine's fast spin whining an accompaniment.

"I've met…" Mal started.

"I've just remembered…" Erin spoke at the same time. They laughed. Erin said, "You first."

"Yeah, sorry. I was about to say I've met some twins at university. Two really nice guys, David and Saul. Spitting image of each other. Hard to tell them apart."

"What do they study?" Erin asked, interested in wanting to know more.

"Dave's doing physics and Saul maths. Very bright – much brighter than me. Anyway, why I mentioned them is that they were kept apart for the first five years of their lives. Didn't know the other existed."

Ice trickled down her spine. Erin shivered in response. She waited for Mal to explain more.

"They grew up in Yorkshire. Saul was sent to a

special school. He doesn't remember much apart from the headteacher always wore purple."

Erin gasped and then calmed herself. Don't be silly – lots of people wear purple.

Mal was continuing. "One other thing he clearly remembers is…" he paused as though for dramatic effect. "…the school was underground, there were only a few children there and his number – A49."

"But they're older than me if they're at university."

"They're 21. They've had a few health issues between them, so they had to take some time out from school." Mal scrambled to his knees and crawled over to the washing machine. He hauled out a mass of twisted pale pink clothes, exclaiming, "What the? This is my white rugby kit and sheets. What's happened to them?"

"I think this is your culprit," announced Erin pulling out the offending red pair of boxers.

"Now what do I do?"

"What's all the noise?" a voice came from beyond the room. Their father's sleepy face appeared in the doorway.

"Mal was just dying his clothes!" giggled Erin.

"Why? What for? Do you know what time it is?" Patrick rubbed his face.

"I didn't mean to, but these were hiding in the machine." Mal pointed at the boxers.

"What are you doing with those? They're

mine!" Patrick explained, his voice rising.

"Patrick – are you okay? I heard voices." Stella arrived, looking pale without makeup, her hair all over the place. Erin glanced at her mum, ready for an angry reaction. Nothing. "Oh, Mal. Leave that now. We'll do it in the morning."

Erin raised her eyebrows and muttered under her breath, "Butter won't melt."

"What's that Erin?" Stella asked, leaving the room with Patrick and Mal in tow.

"Nothing, Mum." Erin sighed, pulled herself up by the cupboard door handles and followed them out.

Frankie – notes from Zephyr tablet

TRIALS

Trials began in the 1990's.

Five sets of twins were separated in 1994 and monitored until 1999. They were contained within Aqua school in Yorkshire.

(I'm not sure of the locality yet. I couldn't find details on the tablet. I think these are the twins Mal met at university. It would be useful to find out if they remember anything else).

Trefoil are part of a large company who trade under the name of Pro-Di-To. They own other subsidiary companies.

Pro-Di-To have their main office in London. Their CEO is a man called Oliver Irons, educated at Eton and Cambridge. He has friends in the government and is a billionaire. (Couldn't find details of how he made his money).

Subsidiary companies are:

Sail Away – boat design and construction.
Flame Fireworks – designers and manufacturers of fireworks

Chapter 7

Music pulsated, lights flashed red and green, yellow and blue, and in their glow, the many twisted faces and gyrating figures were a little frightening to Miranda. She had never experienced anything like this before, and she wasn't sure if she enjoyed it. Standing at the edge of the dance space, she was an outsider to this mob squirming and writhing to the heavy beats, and for a moment or two, she was transported, in her mind, back to Zephyr and the final 'experiment'. The excruciating pain from the constant noise and then unending silence where your ears would throb, and your blood would hammer through your veins.

Suddenly, the music stopped, and the fluorescent tubing high above in the ceiling of the vast farm building was slammed on. The monstrous entity of many heads, arms and legs froze and gradually became detached, shedding into separate beings. Miranda took an immediate intake of breath. She recognised some of the people there. They were people she had seen in Zephyr. Or perhaps replicas, she mused, checking out their hair.

It worked, she thought. This is incredible. I really didn't believe Erin could do this, but she has. As she thought of her sister, Erin's voice flowed to her, and she turned as the crowd also turned as one towards the speaker. Erin was standing on a raised platform before the DJ's mixing desk. She held a microphone to her lips.

"Thank you for coming here tonight. You won't believe how much this means to me… to us." Erin reached out her hand towards Miranda. She beckoned her to join her, and Miranda made her way round the strangely silent people to take her place next to Erin.

"We will return to the music very soon." Erin's comment caused someone to cheer and another to emit a piercing whistle. For a moment, Erin faltered before she raised her head with defiance, and Miranda felt a surge of pride in her chest.

"We would like to explain why you've come here tonight," Erin continued.

"To dance. What else?" A shrill voice came from the centre of the crowd.

Erin nodded, and Miranda could see her knuckles whitening as she tightened her hold of the mic. "My name is Erin, and this is Miranda, my twin sister. I'm sorry if some of you have come here tonight, and you're not affected by what we're about to tell you, but we had to do something."

A few gruff and high-pitched complaints sprang from the mass of people in front of her, and Miranda could sense an unease around the room. Chains clinked on the metal bars sectioning off areas for livestock. People were becoming restless, just like the cattle that usually resided here.

"I never knew I had a twin until last year when I entered a strange school hidden beneath the moors in Cornwall. Miranda had been sent there as a baby and was educated in a similar way to you and I but also very different."

"What's this got to do with us?" shouted a girl, tossing vibrant, blue hair behind rather square shoulders.

Even with all the make-up and piercings, Miranda knew immediately who this was or at least who her twin was. Grabbing the mic from Erin, she replied to the girl. "I know your sister... your TWIN sister!"

"There's only me. I have no siblings," the girl retorted vehemently.

"You were both born on September 1st 2000. She was born at five minutes past three."

The girl's hand flew to her mouth, her eyes wide and questioning. Then she recovered herself. "That's easy to do – you can find out my birthday on the internet."

Miranda continued. "She is known as Z35 Sepcon."

Murmurs and grunts swept around the crowd. Miranda sensed the emotions emanating from the people like an electric shock. She turned towards someone else. "You." She pointed at a boy whose hair lay flat and greasy on his egg-shaped head. He wasn't tall, and his whole demeanour was of an age long past. Instead of jeans, he wore a blazer and tie. Instead of trainers, he wore shoes with spats.

"You…" Miranda repeated, "…were born on December 1st 2000. Your twin was born at fifteen minutes past one. He is known as Z115 Deccon."

The boy frowned and then nodded. "She's right. That's my birthday. I was born at twelve minutes past one, so that makes me the older twin." He puffed out his chest with his own self-importance. "Finally, I am not the youngest in our family."

Miranda repeated the same thing several times over, and each time the mass of people squirmed. Gasps and sighs popping out as more and more were recognised. Miranda paused and handed the mic back to Erin. Exhaustion suddenly washed over her, and tears pricked her eyes.

Erin hugged her tightly. Miranda gulped back the tears. "Tell them what to do," she whispered.

"Some of you may still have doubts. I certainly did, but I have always known from an early age that something in my life was missing. I always felt alone, even in company. I always felt as though I had lost a limb, or my heart wasn't intact. I suffered from aches and pains, and the doctor couldn't find anything wrong with me." Erin's voice rang out loud and clear while everyone stood frozen. No sound came forth from anyone. Just a few nods here and there. Some trying to hold back tears.

"We need your help. Trefoil, the company that runs the four schools, is corrupt and is treating your sibling... your twin, to a horrendous life. We believe from files taken from Zephyr, when we escaped, that their plan is to change our world for their own gratification and their own rise to power. We are led to believe that Trefoil want to rid us of the government and the monarch."

"Good idea, if you ask me." A deep voice boomed from the back of the building.

"No one's asking you, mate," someone on the other side of the bar retorted. Erin smiled as she realised it was Roberto, knowing his political views. "Let her speak."

Erin stood firm, waiting while there was a hush. The silence lay heavy, blanketing the barn.

"Will I get to see my twin sister?" It was the blue-haired girl who Miranda had first spoken to. Erin looked down from the platform and slowly nodded.

"Yes, that is what we want to do. We want to reunite you with your twin if we can."

"Then, I will do anything you ask of me. Tell us what to do."

The many nods and voices assenting to help, created a ripple and then a flow of noise rose to a torrent of shouts and cries.

A sudden banging of metal against metal brought the sound shuddering to stillness again. Erin held aloft a padlock she had left by the side of the stage earlier when they arrived. "We don't have much time left before we must leave this place. We've set up a website. Please click on the fluttering blue butterfly and upload your details and a picture of yourself. If you don't have a phone, then make your way to the tables set out on your right-hand side, where you will find cards and pens. My friends Petra, Rob, Nadir and Willow, will help you. Write down your details so we can contact you when you're needed for our next action against Trefoil. Thank you for coming here tonight. Enjoy some music while you wait."

The DJ started up again, and gradually, people began to form queues at the tables while others stood or sat in small groups studying their phones. Erin felt a small hand take hers, and she looked to her left. It was Miranda. "This is going to work, isn't it?" Miranda spoke softly but loud enough for Erin to hear and to respond.

"Let's hope so. We just need to work out what to do next."

"Do you think they'll come?" Miranda asked.

"Rob said he'd asked his friends, who live at the farm, to phone at around 10pm." Erin's phone lit up as she pressed her thumb on the screen. "It's 11pm. They should be here soon. Farmers are notorious for not liking raves. If they haven't phoned, someone else will have. There are cars parked all up the lane, so that should make the locals suspicious."

"Well done, Erin," Mal said, coming over to stand in front of them. "You too, Miranda – that was amazing what you did there. You're quite a team."

Erin and Miranda grinned. "I just hope this works," Erin murmured.

"Whatever happens – you've set the wheels in motion," Mal replied.

"Absolutely," agreed Miranda. "Little steps, and we'll get there."

When the police arrived, ready to sort out noisy drug and alcohol-fuelled teenagers, they were surprised to find lines of young people patiently waiting to give their details while others sat on the concrete floor of the barn filling in cards or studying phones. Music was playing, but not loud enough to cause a nuisance.

Erin and Mal were waiting at the door to welcome them in. There were two officers, both in uniform, one young and keen, the other more mellow and laid back.

"Good evening," Mal said. "Can we help you?"

"We were informed of an illegal rave going on here at Marsh Lane Farm." It was the young officer who barked out their introduction. He started to prowl around, taking in all his surroundings.

"Hold on lad." The older one stopped his colleague. "Let's check on the facts before we barge in." The young officer halted dead in his tracks and glowered at his teammate.

"Right then. I'm Sergeant Marston. This is PC Latimer. What're your names?" His voice was thick with an accent. Erin tried to place it. Irish perhaps, she thought.

Erin explained they were just kids having a bit of fun and finished by telling them the farmer had allowed them the use of his barn. The younger man didn't seem impressed by their explanation and kept interrupting them. He was like a dog pulling to get off his leash, ready to pounce, wanting to attack.

"Sarge, I'm going to look around."

"Yes, I think we're ready to ask some more questions. Thanks a million, Erin, Malachi. You've been very helpful."

The DJ quickly turned off the music when PC Latimer shouted at him to do so, and an eerie silence descended. The two figures in black wound their way around the barn, stopping now and again to ask questions. Stilted conversations grew once the two men moved onto another group, as though they were dropping seeds of doubt into the minds of the throng of people. Finally, the sergeant returned to the barn's main doors where Erin and Mal had remained like sentries guarding the entrance.

"How'd everyone arrive here tonight, Erin?" he asked, taking off his cap and wiping his forehead, beaded with sweat.

"I'm not entirely sure, but I guess they either drove, had lifts or used public transport."

"Well, we need everyone to disperse. Can some of 'em bed down in here 'til morning?"

Erin nodded. "Sure, they can. Before they all go, do you mind me speaking to everyone?"

"No, go ahead." The sergeant grinned, showing a row of imperfect teeth like fallen gravestones in a churchyard. "My daughter's a similar age to you. I don't think she'd be brave enough to talk to so many people, though."

Erin made her way back to the makeshift stage, where the DJ was busy packing up. The mic had been put away, so Erin grabbed the padlock and banged it against one of the solid black cases that lay ready to ensconce equipment.

"Everyone! Can I have your attention please?" Erin waited for silence. "Thank you for coming here this evening. Thank you for making long journeys. Thank you for believing in us." She took a deep breath. It's now or never, she thought. We have to let the police know what has really happened here tonight. Letting out her breath, her voice wavered momentarily and then grew in strength. "As we said earlier, many of you are a twin who has never met your sibling. You never knew they existed until tonight." Erin glanced across to the two police officers, both standing straight with their hands behind their backs.

"Together, we will rise up against Trefoil, and we will stop their cruel methods of indoctrination, their abuse of power and their treasonous aims." The police sergeant flinched at this. The constable was checking his watch, obviously impatient to get rid of these people, Erin thought. She kept on going. She had never liked speaking in front of her class at school, but now she could feel confidence running through her. She knew this was the only way to make people do something.

"We believe that Trefoil are planning to overthrow our government by murdering them and the Queen in 2018. Trefoil have set up these four schools, Zephyr, Terra, Aqua and Ignis, to create a new race of people who will help them in their quest to change our country into a dictatorship." Erin paused again and stared directly at the police sergeant before continuing.

"We called you here tonight to fight for our country, to fight for our young people and to protect us in our fight."

"Where's your evidence of this?" PC Latimer yelled, his weaselly face pinched with distrust.

"We have plenty of evidence," replied Erin. "But we need your help in getting this shown to the proper authorities."

Sergeant Marston started to make his way towards Erin. "That's enough. You need to be careful about making wild allegations." He stopped and turned towards the crowd.

"They're part of Pro-Di-To!" someone shouted. Erin felt her heart lift. It was Miranda.

"What did you say?" asked Latimer.

"Trefoil are part of Pro-Di-To, the international pharmaceutical company. They use their company name to appear legitimate. They are engineering fireworks to cause mass destruction of the Houses of Parliament." Miranda's voice surged over the astonished audience, whose gasps of horror added fuel to Miranda's statement.

Someone shouted, "NO!" and it acted like a taper lighting the fuse of anger and frustration.

"That's not right."

"They can't do that."

"You're lying!"

Accusations were now being fired at Erin and Miranda like firecrackers. Words exploded around them.

"It's like Guy Fawkes all over again." This last remark was from PC Latimer, creating laughter and snorts of derision. "Like the Sergeant has said, you can't throw these allegations around. You might find it all might explode in your face." He guffawed at his own pun.

Miranda's voice became more urgent. "It's all true. Every word we have told you tonight is the truth. You must believe us. Please."

"We've heard enough, young lady. Your little call to arms is over." Latimer barked out orders. "Those of you who have transport, make your way to your car. Anyone who can't travel until the morning can stay here. We'll come back at 8am to make sure everyone's dispersed."

Erin looked around her at the sea of faces. She felt completely deflated by the policemen's reactions. "I'm sorry we don't have any blankets and stuff but make yourselves as comfortable as possible."

Various groups of people made their way to the entrance and disappeared into the night while the rest settled down in little knots of three or four, some leaning back against the cold steel fencing that was scattered around the barn while others used their bags and jackets as pillows.

The policemen left, saying they would be contacting parents in the morning.

That was the final nail in the coffin, and Miranda and Erin slumped down on the floor, dejected. They were soon joined by Petra, Mal, Rob, Nadir and Willow. "You look exhausted," Willow said, bobbing her head at Erin.

"I'm sorry, Erin. It was stupid of me," Rob blurted out. "Next time I come up with some crazy suggestion, just tell me to shut up."

"No, it was a good idea," Erin said softly. "We had to do something. Let's get some sleep."

When Erin stirred from a dreamless, uncomfortable sleep of about two hours, she saw that most of the crowd had left. There were only a few piles of people haphazardly strewn across the concrete floor. Her stomach growled, reminding her she hadn't eaten since early last night, and she craved a cup of coffee. Checking the time on her phone, she saw it was time to get moving; the police would be back soon. Rubbing her eyes, she struggled to sit up and realised that a denim jacket had been placed over her as a makeshift blanket. It smelt comfortingly of Nadir's aftershave, and she smiled at the figure curled up next to her, his arms wrapped around himself to keep warm. She laid the jacket over his sleeping form and clambered to her feet.

Her muscles felt tight and stiff, and she hobbled about trying to get them moving. The aroma of coffee unexpectedly wafted over, and she looked up to see Roberto with a tray full of mugs of coffee and tea.

"Sandy let me into the kitchen. I thought I would start making amends by getting you some caffeine."

Erin wrapped her hands around a substantial earthenware mug, the heat radiating into her hands and arms and finally her whole body. "No need to make amends, Rob. But I won't say no to coffee."

Rob kicked Nadir's boots to wake him before planting the tray down and wrapping his arms around Willow. She kissed him sleepily, and he stroked her face. Erin turned away, leaving them to their morning cuddle and took some refreshment over to the others.

"Excuse me." A small voice came from behind her, and Erin turned. There was a group of four standing there. "We just wanted to say thank you for last night. We're right behind you – literally…" the girl sniggered. It was the blue-haired girl.

"Yeah. We're ready to do anything to help. Just text us and let us know what our next step is," another one added.

At the word, *our*, Erin's heart soared. "Really? You want to help us?" Erin asked.

"Of course. We were talking last night after the cops left. We want to know about our twins. We've all suspected something for a long time, and last night we were able to share those worries with each other. I'm known as Blue by the way." She gestured towards her hair.

The other three began introducing themselves, but further discussion was cut off by the barn door banging as it was thrown open. The two policemen strode in accompanied by Stella and Patrick, who proceeded to rush over to Erin and Miranda, their faces white with anger.

"We'll get going." The set of four trudged across to the door and disappeared.

Hope rushed through Erin, yet soon evaporated as Stella screamed at them. "You said you were sleeping over at Willow's. What the hell are you all doing here?"

Everyone waited as Stella railed. "You are all inconsiderate, immature and thoughtless people. What were you thinking?"

"Mal?" Patrick said. "I never thought you would be involved in something as ridiculous as a rave. Erin yes, but you!"

Anger bubbled inside her, and Erin was about to retort when Mal spoke. His voice strong and confident.

"It wasn't a rave, Dad. Whatever the police have told you, they're wrong. We needed to do something to…"

Erin was horrified; he was going to tell them. She had to stop him, he didn't know their mother, and possibly their father was involved with Trefoil.

Grabbing at Mal's elbow she finished his sentence. "…to celebrate our last chance to enjoy ourselves before revision and exams. Yes, it's my fault. I put them all up to it." She raised both hands in submission. "You can punish me, but the others are innocent."

She looked around the huddle of people, praying no one would say anything. Mal frowned at her questioning her confession. She gave a tiny shake of the head, and he responded with a raised eyebrow.

"Yeah. As you can see it was just a bit of a party," Mal added lamely.

"That's as maybe," countered Patrick. "But the police are now involved, and all the parents are waiting outside. They're like us – very disappointed in your actions."

↩ Reply   ↩ Reply all   → Forward   ▭ Archive   • • •

Parent Feedback

PW   Patrick Winslow <patrick.winslow@hotmail.co.uk>
        10:41

To: Professor Mallory

Dear Professor Mallory,

As I said in our recent video call, I received some replies from parents of the Teardrops. Below are some examples. I was concerned that most of them were very negative and quite hostile towards me.

Obviously since sending the letters out all the children have returned to Zephyr, but I feel that with your help we can contact more parents and explain to them what is really going on with Trefoil and Pro-Di-To. May I suggest at our next video call we discuss this in detail with the others.

Kind regards,

Patrick Winslow

Patrick Winslow

Some replies:

Jem Stone - Return our son at once. You have no right to do this.

Fiora Norton - You must be mad - I am living the life of luxury and I am not prepared to lose that due to my child. Take her back immediately.

Jay Kemsey senior - I trust Trefoil implicitly. I visit my son every 5 years and he is well and healthy and has much better manners than my other children.

Alice Blake - Please let me know more about this. I want to help but I'm very scared. Please text me.

Chapter 8

 Miranda was instantly awake. Someone was in her room.

"Who is it? What do you want?" she asked, her voice husky with sleep.

"Shhh. It's only me." It was Erin.

Miranda leaned over to switch on her bedside lamp. "What time is it?" She yawned.

"About 7.15... in the evening. We've slept all day." Erin perched on the side of the bed. "I'm so sorry."

"What for?"

"I've made a real mess of everything. Mum and Dad are furious about last night. Now we're grounded, and I don't know what to do." Erin's snuffled voice suggested she had been crying, and Miranda laid her hand on her sister's arm.

"There's nothing to be sorry about. As you said last night... this morning... whenever it was... we had to try something. Anyway, our little band of four are going to help us."

Erin scoffed. "Oh yeah. Four against the world. That's going to end well."

Miranda was puzzled. She didn't recognise this Erin. Her sister was always so positive. "This isn't like you."

"This is the real me. The me you've not met before—the me who is weak and pathetic and who doesn't believe in herself. I thought I could change the world. What an idiot!"

"Losing one battle doesn't mean you've lost the war."

Erin glared at her sister. "Since when have you become an orator?"

Miranda grinned at this. "Since I realised you were such a wuss." She grabbed one of the many cushions that were scattered around the bed and hit Erin with it. For a second time stood still. And in that second, Erin's face went from sad to astonished.

"What the?"

Miranda thought, perhaps I've gone too far. Erin had risen, taken another cushion, and Miranda waited.

"Oh. It's like that, is it?" Erin said. Miranda stared back; there was sudden menace in her grey eyes. Then, just like the sun coming out from behind storm clouds, Erin's face cracked into a broad grin. "Come on then." Miranda found herself being gently pummelled with the soft feathery cushion.

This must be what they call play fighting, she

thought. I'm not going to lie here and be attacked. She rolled away from the firing line, her cushion raised for another attack and was instantly taken off guard. More cushions lay on the floor where Miranda had landed, and using the bed as her protection, she began to throw her soft fluffy missiles. Most of them missed. Then one hit Erin square in the face.

"Ow!"

Miranda peeped over the bed. "I'm the winner!" she yelled before diving back to safety when her own missile returned back, skimming the top of her head.

A shrill cry from the doorway announced the arrival of Stella. "What are you two doing? STOP IT! NOW!"

Miranda and Erin crept out from their respective hiding places, their imaginary trenches. No Man's Land, AKA the bed, was a wreck of twisted duvet and battered pillows and cushions.

"You're not children anymore. It's time you took some responsibility, especially after last night. God only knows what you've taken. Some weird stuff. I blame Roberto as well as you. He told us this morning it had been his idea. I've a good mind to go and speak to his parents." Stella was on a roll now. There was no dodging the explosion of accusations.

"You need to come downstairs. The police are here to ask you some questions. You can sort this out later and for goodness' sake, get dressed." At this, she turned and left the room.

Miranda gazed at her sister. Erin spoke. "Looks like we've released the beast." Her eyes shone wide, and a smile played across her mouth. They collapsed into each other's arms giggling, the absolute joy of being sisters, twins, friends wrapped its arms around them and held them tight. They were a team once again.

Sergeant Marston was waiting to speak with them, a mug of steaming tea set on the kitchen's breakfast bar.

"Good evening Erin, Miranda," he said. He was out of uniform, dressed casually in jeans and chequered shirt. A green fleeced jacket lay on the stool next to him.

The girls said good evening and remained standing. Stella hovered near them, Miranda sensing her mother's disquiet.

"Thank you, Mrs Winslow. I'd like to talk to the girls alone if that's all right with you," Marston said, his tone softening.

"Oh. They're only sixteen. I'm not sure about that."

"They'll be all right with me. They're not being charged or anything like that. I just want to give them some advice."

"Okay. Well, that's good to hear. I'll be in my study if you need me." With that, Stella turned and left the room, shutting the door behind her.

Birdsong from beyond the kitchen window,

caught her attention, something so simple and often unnoticed, but for her, it meant she was free. Miranda's heart hammered as if to escape. *What is he going to say?*

"Sit down girls. Don't worry. You both look terrified. The farmer's not pressing any charges. They said they had offered the space to you. There was no sign of drugs. A few bottles of beer and cider but nothing too incriminating. So, you're off the hook." Miranda and Erin both let out pent up air they had been holding onto.

Sergeant Marston laughed. A warm, chocolatey laugh. He beamed and then, draining his mug, said, "I could do with another one of those and perhaps a biscuit or two. What do you say we put the kettle on and have a proper chat? I want to tell you something."

 Fresh tea made and biscuits offered, they settled down to talk. "What I'm about to tell you… I've never told anyone else… I don't know where to start." Marston's voice trailed away.

He was silent for a moment. Then lifting his mug to his mouth, he slurped the liquid noisily. "Sorry," he said. "My daughter's always telling me off for that. Sensitive lips, you know."

Erin beat her fingers on the marble worktop. Why are we wasting time with this? I wanted to watch that movie tonight. Her body language must have signalled something to the man because he started to speak. "She does that too. Especially when her daft father's being slow and boring."

"Oh, sorry. I didn't mean to…"

"No, I'm sorry. This needs to be said, so I will just come out with it. We couldn't have children – my wife and I. Beth became desperate. Hated herself every month. Thought she was letting me down. Anyway, someone approached us at a clinic and said they could help us. They would pay for the IVF treatment and help us out financially."

"What does this have to do with us?" Miranda asked.

"We discovered we were having twins at the twelve-week scan. We were then informed that we had signed a contract agreeing if we were expecting twins, for one child to be taken away to be educated at a special school. Beth and I were horrified, as you can imagine. We checked the contract, and there in the small print, there was a section stating exactly that. I don't see how we missed it, but there it was in black and white."

Erin's vision wavered as though she had been spun round and round on a Wurlitzer. "Where's the school?" she croaked.

"It's called Aqua School... it's in Yorkshire... we visit her every five years... her name is Daisy. We're not allowed to tell her who we are." His lilting Irish accent cracked and splintered. "She's... she is... beautiful."

Erin and Miranda gaped at the man. His hooded eyes were full of sadness and regret. A sudden shout from the doorway made them all start.

"Are you going to be much longer?" It was Stella. Erin stared back at her mother, who was standing with her hands on her hips. "These girls need to eat." As if the dinner itself was getting impatient too, a meaty aroma wafted through the kitchen.

"Smells nice, Mrs Winslow."

"It won't be if you keep them much longer," Stella said testily.

"Mum. Can you just give us five minutes?" Erin asked in her sweetest voice.

Stella grunted, whipped round and stomped back to her study.

"We don't have much time," Erin whispered. "Our mum and dad mustn't know about this."

"But surely they're in the same situation as Beth and me," urged Sergeant Marston.

"No, we can't tell them," Miranda agreed. "We suspect they're working for Trefoil."

The policeman frowned. Then his face cleared. "Here's my card. You can come and meet Imogen, our other daughter. After what you said at your so-called rave, I want to help. I want my Daisy back home." He pushed his fingers through thinning hair before sliding his large frame off the bar stool.

At the door, he turned, "I'll be in touch. I'll see myself out. Good night." With that, he left the room. The front door slammed, and Miranda and Erin were left perched on their respective stools.

Erin looked searchingly at her sister. "Wow! I wasn't expecting that."

"Me neither," Miranda said.

Before they could talk further, Stella bustled into the room, threw open the oven door and called them to help sort the table out for dinner.

"Hi Frankie. How are you?" Erin asked. She leaned back against the cold resistance of one of the upright stones in the Seven Spirits, holding her phone out so Miranda could see the screen.

"Hi. Yeah, I'm good, thanks. How are you?" Frankie's face had filled out a little and his red hair curled around his ears. Elsie was obviously looking after him, she thought.

Miranda gave a little wave, and Frankie returned a Teardrop sign. Erin could sense the excitement of her twin at seeing the boy she loved so much, her face in the tiny rectangle at the top of the screen radiating her joy. Was he just as pleased to see her as she is to see him? Erin wondered.

"Pandora and Edward are here too," Frankie explained, turning the screen to show them.

"That's brilliant!" exclaimed Erin. They exchanged hellos.

"Is it safe to talk?" asked Pandora.

"Yes, we're away from the house. We should be okay here," replied Erin.

"What have you got to report?" asked Frankie.

Erin and Miranda between them described the rave and then the consequences of meeting the police. They left their final revelation to the last. Erin was bubbling with excitement when she told of what Sergeant Marston had revealed to them about his daughter being at Aqua School.

"When are you seeing him and his daughter?" Pandora asked.

"Tomorrow. They live over in Milton, but we're meeting them in Newton at a coffee shop." Erin went on to explain their plans. "Sergeant Marston has said he will do anything he can to help us."

Frankie started lobbing questions at Erin and Miranda. How many parents replied to the letters Patrick posted last Summer? What about Stella — have you seen her with anyone from Zephyr or Trefoil? What about Patrick? Can we trust him?

Erin fielded most of the questions, with Miranda adding a few comments here and there. No, they hadn't seen Stella communicate with Esme Dorling and their Aunt Angela again. They weren't sure about their father, and no, they hadn't asked him about the letters. They confessed to checking Patrick's phone while it was charging one night and hurriedly described some of the messages they found. The majority of parents weren't interested in bringing their child out of Zephyr; they were enjoying the financial benefits too much. It was another dead end.

The girls paused — Frankie wasn't impressed with their answers. His face was like thunder. Before he could say anything, Erin tossed a back-handed comment into the mix.

"Mal's met some students from the Aqua school in Yorkshire."

Erin was pleased to see Frankie's discomfort. His eyes narrowed and he asked for more clarification. Erin took great pleasure in passing on Mal's news about the twins in York. He had been told to return to university with Patrick's angry remonstrances still ringing in his ears. You should have stopped them. You're the mature, sensible one here and so on.

Erin finished her explanation by saying, "Also, they're going to take him to see where it is." She sat back feeling smug, but the feeling soon evaporated.

"Well, it's not a lot, is it. Better than nothing I suppose."

Edward's face suddenly loomed large on the phone screen. "There have been some interesting developments at Zephyr," he said mysteriously before disappearing.

Frankie's face now came into full view. His eyes swivelled back the way Edward had gone and then focused back on the girls. His face was set in an earnest frown.

"Thanks for that, Edward. We need to update you. Amber, as you know, is our eyes and ears in there. She attended a conference with all the teachers and principals of the four schools at Trefoil HQ."

Erin feeling a little more relaxed, giggled, "That must have been quite a sight. A rainbow of colours."

Miranda joined in. "A kaleidoscope of colour," she mused.

"Yes, well anyway. Let's focus, shall we?" Frankie was blunt. "Amber said they're planning a run-through named Operation Firework this November in preparation for 2018 when the final plan, named *Paper Boats and Butterflies*, goes operational."

Erin and Miranda huddled together, their moment of wit and mirth vanishing into the air around them – a sparkle of joy turning into a damp squib with the feeling of impending doom. Frankie filled them in with details of what they had found so far.

Frankie threw a question at them. "How many people do you think can help us?"

Erin did some quick mental arithmetic and then said in a husky voice. "Probably about 27." On seeing Frankie's scowl, she muttered, "Perhaps, 30-35. I'm sorry it's not more, but I'm not sure if we can count on everyone who came to the rave."

"Well, that will have to do, for now at any rate." Frankie sighed and then said in a more hopeful tone, "We will trust in exponential growth. That number will grow. I know it will."

"What's our next move?" asked Pandora.

"Yes. What is our next move, Erin? More parties? More fun and cheer?" Frankie was scornful, his tone bitter.

A sudden angry heat coursed through her body. She was fed up with Frankie's negativity. "You think it's so easy, don't you? You think you can escape from Zephyr and save the world just like that!" She clicked her fingers on her final word.

"We still have to go to school; we still have to pretend to Mum and Dad we're doing what Trefoil have asked us to do. I don't have all the answers. I don't know how we can stop this huge company Pro-Di-To from pouring money into this insane idea of ending our world as we know it and ultimately becoming governed by them and their minions." Her voice was growing shriller with every syllable, her frustration deepening with every nuance. Erin stopped her diatribe, breathing hard and fast. She spat her final blow at the screen. "Frankie – you can lead us from now on. I'm sick and tired of you."

"Erin!" It was Miranda. She had placed her hand on Erin's arm at some time during this tirade, and her grip was now tightening. "We cannot fight amongst ourselves. If we do, then they've won." She lightened her hold, and Erin turned, her frustration dissolving. Her shoulders drooped, and a weariness washed over her.

"I can't do this anymore. I just want my normal life back," she whispered.

Miranda's eyes grew round, and her cheeks reddened. "I will go back to Zephyr. Then we can continue as normal."

Erin's heart skipped a beat. "No. I didn't mean that 'normal'. No. You can't leave me. I need you. I've been searching for you all my life."

Miranda was on her feet in an instant, her expression set and stumbled towards the altar stone. Erin jumped to her feet, her phone tumbling down onto the grass, and ran after her sister, who was now hiccupping with loud sobs.

"I didn't mean for you to go back." Erin's shout

was caught by a wind that had appeared from nowhere, and her words flew high into the sky. "Miranda, come back. Please. It's just me and my silly confidence. I never believe in myself; I don't believe I can change the world. What can one person do?"

"I don't want to go back to Zephyr. I just want you to be happy." Miranda turned to face Erin. "You're not on your own – we're a team, you and I. Together we can do this."

High above them, a rumble rolled within the gathering army of clouds. The sky was now granite. The girls stopped as one and looked upwards into the gloom until a sudden flash of lightning streaked across the heavens heralding the final gift of rain. Fat dollops of water dropped on the grass surrounding them, splashed into their eyes and then for an encore, as though on a film set when the hose pipes had been turned on, the rain lashed down, hammering against their slim bodies.

"Quick," shouted Erin, her allegedly waterproof mascara running down her pale skin. "There's a shelter in the next field. It'll be quicker than running home." She grabbed Miranda's arm to steer her away from the Seven Spirits, through a gate and into a lean-to stone building hugging the hedge.

The smell was rather pungent – a mixture of animal faeces and human urine – and the earth floor was littered with dead fag ends. "What is this place?" asked Miranda, shivering violently.

"I think it's where the shepherd used to rest years ago. Now it's shared by the sheep and local teenagers." Erin hugged her sister and rubbed her arms hard to bring some warmth. She let go and peered through the fourth wall, open to the elements. Nature continued its show – bright forked lightning lit up the fields like a stage while thunder clapped wildly at the straight-down rain falling in perfect unison. A shadow entered downstage right and almost fell into Erin and Miranda's arms.

The dripping figure stumbled and muttered a sorry. Pulling its hood back and shaking its head, the soggy mass materialised into Nadir.

Erin's frozen body warmed at the sight of him. "Hey, you had the same idea," she exclaimed.

"Obviously." Nadir grinned. "It's coming down in torrents."

"Raining cats and dogs," added Erin.

Miranda looked blank. "Where?"

"Where what?"

"I don't see any dogs or cats."

Erin giggled. "It's just an expression."

"I was on my way to see you. Your mum told me you were at the Spirits, so I came looking for you. Then the storm came, and I remembered this place. Hey, I found this." Nadir thrust out his hand with Erin's phone perched on top.

"Thanks, Nad. What would I do without you?" Erin said, taking the phone, looking directly into her friend's face. He returned the stare, and Erin turned away at the same time as Nadir began a coughing fit. Her hands shook as she tried to get her phone to spring to life, but nothing. The rain had put it to sleep.

"Rice."

"Sorry, what?" Erin asked, her gaze still focused on her blank screen.

"Rice," repeated Nadir. "When you get home, put it in a bowl of rice to dry."

Erin glanced up. "It's okay. I know what to do. This is my third time of soaking phones. Once down the loo and now twice in the rain."

"Yuck!" Miranda gasped. "That's disgusting."

"Yeah, tell me about it." Erin paused as she removed the sim card. "I need to dry it off as much as possible before that."

"Maybe I can help after all." Nadir pulled his rucksack off his shoulder and rummaged around in one of the many pockets. "Use this." He handed her a packet of tissues.

"You should have been a boy scout. You're always prepared for every eventuality. Thanks, Nad," Erin said, taking the proffered pack.

The three of them settled down on the cold damp earth floor of the hut. Erin set upon carefully drying her phone and its cover. She pocketed them along with the sim card wrapped in tissue. Meanwhile, Nadir had been removing various goodies from his bag. "Survival rations," he murmured, handing over chocolate bars to the girls.

They munched in silence, staring at the rain; emerald grass and nutbrown earth blurring and blending into a watercolour painting.

Miranda spoke first. "Erin and I were talking about being together, helping each other before the storm came. She doesn't believe in herself."

Erin shifted her eyes sideways to her twin, unsure of where this was going.

"I know she doesn't," agreed Nadir, through a mouthful of chocolate. "I think we all go through that at times. I get it when I'm auditioning for a play or school musical. And then at the end of a show, the applause is just great, so I know I did well. But it's not just that. It's about overcoming your fears. As an only child in a mixed-race family, I've had a few battles to fight – mental and physical. Other kids making fun of my parents and me. People commenting on my uncle and his funny ways. It's important to only show your weakness to those you love and who love you. If you can love yourself, then you can believe in yourself." He popped another piece of chocolate in his mouth to stop himself from talking.

Erin smiled inwardly. He never opens up about his feelings. It's true what he says – we are all hard on ourselves, much harder than on anyone else.

The chocolate hadn't had the desired effect on stalling Nadir, and he went on. "I think you're amazing, Erin. You found your sister; you've stood up to people, and you've changed the lives of many. You can do this…" he broke off and shovelled in his last piece.

"He's right, Erin," soothed Miranda. "But you're not on your own. We can do this together. We need to get a plan of action that works and see this through to the bitter end."

Erin nodded. "Wow, you two. You're ganging up on me now." She took a deep breath. "Yes, we need a plan… as soon as I've finished my chocolate and the rain stops."

Nature obliged. The storm shifted, the rain subsided, and the sky melded into a silvery grey. Erin blinked and obediently ate her last chunk. Before she could change her mind, the others were on their feet and pulling her up.

Returning to the Seven Spirits, they were shocked to see a giant oak tree split in half by the storm. Lightning had overpowered it, and now one section of the trunk leaned heavily on one of the Spirits, so much so the rock had been pushed almost flat against the ground. Erin cried out at the devastation of her special place, and while Miranda comforted her, Nadir strode across to inspect the damage.

"Hey. Come and look at this," he shouted. Hurrying over to where Nadir stood, Erin and

Miranda could see what had caused his burst of excitement. Where the Spirit rock had been levered up by the tree, a crack had formed in the mud. A musty, sour odour reached out to them and water, dripping away the seconds, swelled about their feet.

"Perhaps Uncle Jim was right after all. This could be a tunnel leading down inside the hill." Nadir knelt and started to scrabble at the loose earth around the gash in the ground.

"Nadir, stop. You're getting filthy," Erin cried. The boy continued to dig, ignoring her.

Erin threw her arms in the air. "Boys? I'll never understand them." She knew when she was beaten. "I'll go and find a spade or something from our shed. Miranda, can you stay here and make sure the idiot doesn't fall in and get swallowed up by the earth?"

"Swallowed up?" Miranda's eyes were dark chasms, just like Erin's imaginings.

"Not literally." Erin laughed. "Just a figure of speech. I won't be long." Erin trudged towards the entrance to the field, where she turned and waved.

Making her way across the road to her house and down the drive, she was surprised to see a sleek black car parked. She bobbed her head to the side as she passed it and saw a driver sitting reading a newspaper.

Erin went to go around to the back garden to investigate the shed, the interior of which she had little knowledge, but she thought it was probably where the gardener kept his tools. Almost on cue, the front door opened, and Stella materialised. "Where have you been? I've been worried sick. Where's Miranda?"

"Sorry, Mum. We got stuck in the storm and sheltered in the old sheep shed. Are you okay?"

Erin felt a coldness take hold. Afterwards, she thought, why hadn't she been ready for this? Why hadn't she fled when she saw the car? But at this moment, her mother beckoned her inside and like a lamb happily going to an unknown slaughter, she obeyed.

Trefoil HQ Conference
Notes on Power Point
Amber Hessonite

2016
The River Thames Celebrations.

Pro-Di-To will be the main sponsors of this
huge event. Various re-enactments from history
as well as performances by dancers, choirs
and actors will be staged along from The Tower
of London.
Our three subsidiary companies will be staging
their own performance from Westminster
Bridge. Operation Firework will be part of this.

Looking ahead – 2018

Paper Boats & Butterflies

Our CEO will be celebrating his 60th birthday
on 5th November 2018. His aim is to celebrate
this in style and in his words 'to change the
country for the better'. Once Operation Firework
is accomplished, we can move forwards on this

Chapter 9

 Miranda hovered near the kneeling figure of Nadir holding his phone up with the torch shining out. She studied the fractured ground, open-mouthed at what had been revealed by the digging.

The rock below seemed to criss-cross, forming a kind of staircase. Before she could stop him, Nadir had swung his legs over the edge and was beginning to wiggle his lean body down into the widening crevice.

"What are you doing?" she asked, knowing full well what he intended as she could see him begin to slide down and to be swallowed up by the ground, yet her mind was telling her to say something.

"I think if I can get a toehold on the rock, then I might be able to get a better look."

"Shouldn't we wait for Erin?" A sudden gust of wind chilled Miranda, and she rubbed her arms hard. A sudden stabbing pain in her left upper arm caused her to cry out.

"Are you okay?" Nadir shouted, his legs hidden from view, with his upper body seemingly stuck in the hole.

Miranda would have found his predicament amusing if a sudden wooziness hadn't taken over. She reeled, blinking her eyes over and over to clear her vision. A terrifying image of Erin, lying lifeless in a coffin, swam before her. "Erin's in danger. I must go to her." Turning away in confusion, she ran headlong into a solid wall.

The wall spoke and shook her hard. "Miranda. It's me, Dad. Look at me."

Miranda opened her eyes. Patrick's face was two inches from her own, her arms held firmly in his unyielding hands. "Dad. What's happened? Where's Erin?"

Patrick shook her again. "Listen to me," he hissed. "We don't have much time. Erin's been taken by Trefoil."

For Miranda, the Earth stopped revolving. Just for a second. She heard a moan, like a stricken animal. Bewildered, she realised the sound came from her own lips. "Dad? How?"

"They're at the house. I said I would come and get you. They injected her, and she's now asleep in the back of one of their cars." At that, Miranda unconsciously rubbed her arm again where she had felt the sting. "Pandora texted me; they were worried when your phone went dead."

"Pandora? She wasn't to tell you," Miranda said.

Patrick continued. "Pardon? Why couldn't she tell me?" Patrick shook his head. "Anyway, you must hide. Somewhere. Anywhere. I'll tell them I can't find you. What the…?" This final ejaculation was on seeing Nadir struggling out of the mud. "Nadir? What are you doing down there?"

"I think this is one of the Spirit tunnels. Uncle Jim always said there were tunnels up here in the hill and not just under the pubs in town." Nadir slapped his grimy hands against his mud-caked jeans trying unsuccessfully to clear some of the dirt. The force of a body pulling clear created a chain reaction, and the rim of the fissure fell in, displaying several steps carved out of the rock below.

Patrick let go and grabbed the young man's hands. "Take Miranda down there. Hide her. Please."

"Dad, we thought you were on their side," Miranda interrupted.

The horror at Miranda's suggestion shone in Patrick's eyes. "Never!" he protested. "After what they have done to our family. They must be stopped. Now, you must go. Take this." He passed his phone and a bundle of bank notes. "I'll be in touch. Nadir, look after my beautiful girl, won't you?"

Nadir nodded and turned back to the long-dead tunnel entrance, flicking his torch back on to show them the way.

Miranda hugged her father, pushed the notes and phone into a back pocket and then followed Nadir's disappearing form. Before she too was consumed by the ground, her final sight and sound of her father was of him explaining as he heaved the tree towards the pit. "I don't know where this'll take you. I'll block up the entrance with the fallen branches and split trunk. It'll have to do for now. I'll tell them I can't find you and we can't reach you by phone. I'll think of something. Stay safe and strong. I love you, Miranda."

His final words stayed with her, settling her mind until an unpleasant dankness snaked around her flicking its forked tongue, piercing her heart and pulling her breath away for a second or two. She slid and slithered down slippery steps hewn out of the rock before coming to a halt. Blackness devoured her, yet she wasn't frightened. This was nothing compared to what she had endured while in Zephyr. Steadying herself, Miranda continued her descent. She felt inside crevices with her feet and her fingers taking a step at a time. In one abrupt movement, Nadir's torchlight shone upwards, and she paused, looking down. His face was hidden, but she heard his voice clearly.

"I'm at the bottom. You're nearly there now."

Miranda resumed, stepping gingerly, and soon found herself next to Nadir. "Can you get this to work?" she asked, pulling out her father's phone from her pocket.

Nadir passed her his own phone, the torch glowing up into his face, causing a brief ghoulish gleam. While he slid his finger across the black screen to wake it up, Miranda looked around her, the torch illuminating a rocky chamber.

"This is amazing," she said as they swapped phones. "What is this place?"

"You know the legend of the Seven Spirits, don't you?" asked Nadir, shining his torch around them both.

"How could I not? Erin loves The Spirits. They were seven people who danced on the Sabbath and were instantly turned to stone. They said a huge storm created the altar stone."

"Just like our storm has finally shown us this long-forgotten place. Another part of the legend was that the seven would often appear and reappear at this place as if by magic, and that was one reason the village elders feared them. My Uncle Jim has said for years since he began exploring the smugglers' tunnels under his shop that there were more."

"Well, it's a good place to hide from Trefoil for the time being. Shall we see if it goes anywhere?"

Nadir nodded, and the two of them began to search the space. "Here." Miranda looked up to see Nadir pointing at a shadowy cavity. Joining him, she saw it wasn't high enough for them to walk through, and as nothing else resembled any kind of exit, it was their only option. Lowering herself to her hands and knees, she followed Nadir, their two lights brightening the gloom slightly. Gradually the passageway became bigger, with the ceiling creating an archway high enough for them to walk while stooping to prevent bashing their heads. The tunnel shifted downward, and the rock became solid earth shored up in places by wooden beams and planks. The air was stagnant and lifeless. Miranda wondered if anyone else had been down here since medieval times.

The passage made a violent turn to the right and tipped away, the ground becoming uneven. Nadir was disappearing far ahead, and Miranda began to hurry to keep up with him. Suddenly, she caught her foot against a stone and nearly pitched headfirst. Righting herself, she proceeded more slowly.

Nadir's light stopped and then shone to the left. What now? Miranda thought. Catching up with him, she also shone her torch to the left and there in front of them a door made of criss-crossing metal rods barred their way. A rusted padlock and chain twisting through the iron handle showed them they had reached a dead-end.

"So near and yet so far," muttered Nadir.

Miranda sat on her haunches to catch her breath. Tiredness took over, and she slumped against wooden planks set into the wall. "Do you have any more chocolate?" she asked.

In answer, Nadir knelt and, opening his rucksack, began to shuffle through the contents. A packet of bourbon biscuits was thrust onto

Miranda's lap, and a bottle of coke along with a rather squashed bag of crisps soon followed.

"Have you any idea of where we are?" she mumbled after polishing off a few biscuits.

"Not sure, but I think we might be near the church." Nadir scrambled to his feet and shone his torch through the rusting metal bars. It lit up a small cell-like room, bare of furniture.

 Erin woke from a non-dreaming sleep, her whole-body aching. The chill air was biting, and a shiver rippled through her. Where am I? The dense night was suffocating, and for a moment or two, she struggled to breathe. What is this place? Rubbing her eyes and face hard to bring some life into them, she could make out a series of small triangles cut into one wall and open to the elements. Moonlight glowed through these apertures, and as her eyes became more accustomed to the darkness, she could see she was in a stone room with just three walls. One wall held a solid-looking door. Erin struggled to her feet and rattled the iron handle. The door was locked from the outside. Clenching her hands into tight fists, she pounded them against the wood, simultaneously shouting for help.

She paused, panting, listening. No answer came. No sound at all. Erin started up again. Her shouts echoed around her prison, and still nothing. She turned towards the wall with the triangular holes. Choosing the largest shape in the middle of the pattern, she pressed her face against the ice-cold stone surround and looked out. The moon was a huge round ball floating on a sea of wispy clouds. Below were fields and hedges, trees and bushes, all monochrome. A flurry of feathers flashed past her, and an owl swooped down to the ground. In seconds, it was airborne again, with the body of a mouse drooping from its talons.

Erin shivered. She felt as trapped as the tiny mouse. She was miles from anywhere in a strange building and couldn't remember how she had been transported here.

Before her fighting spirit completely waned, she yelled repeatedly into the night air. The only reply was a shrieking cry far across the fields. A fox thought Erin. She tried the door again, twisting the handle back and forth but to no avail. It wasn't budging. She thrashed wildly at the door until all her energy was depleted. Dropping to her hands and knees, her head hanging heavy, she knew there was no escape. Worn out, Erin fell to one side, curled up in a ball and closed her eyes.

A rattling sound roused her, and before she could sit up, the door opened, and a gruff voice ordered, "Get up. You've been summoned."

Scrambling to her feet, Erin peered out at a grey-haired man standing with one hand on the open door and the other nonchalantly in the pocket of his brown uniform. "They ain't got all day. Get movin'."

Erin did as she was told and moved. She found herself in a hexagonal room with intricate patterns cut into stone walls. Before she could take in much more, the man pushed her towards a staircase that spiralled down into nothingness. Using outstretched fingers against the curving wall surrounding the worn steps, she made her way down. Whenever she reached an open doorway, the man prodded her from behind and rasped out orders to keep going down the steps. Finally, they couldn't go any further, and Erin stepped out into an area that seemed incongruous to the gothic architecture above. This is just like Zephyr, she pondered, everywhere white and sterile.

A flickering of gold and red to her right caught her eye. One wall was completely encased with a very fine mesh enclosing an area of trees and plants. A fountain played within, and Erin wondered why this area was closed off. The answer came to her when the flickering began again and again and again until the whole enclosure seemed to be moving with life. A myriad of colour – butterflies of every colour and size rested on the lush green leaves wafting their wings and in that moment Erin's spirits lifted. She adored butterflies, and she made to go closer to study the shimmering insects. A heavy hand on her shoulder drew her back to a desk where a mousy woman in beige was seated facing a computer.

The woman glanced up at their arrival and indicated for Erin to wait while she lifted the handset of a shiny white telephone. "She is here. Shall I send her in, sir?" The woman nodded as though in answer to instructions and then pressed something on her desk, resulting in a door sliding open to her left. Erin waited, her stomach tying itself in knots.

"You may enter The Sanctum." The beige woman gestured to the open doorway, and Erin started forward.

On entering, she recognised the room immediately as the place where she had watched her mother being interrogated by two people in white and a third unseen person. A vast space. Ahead of her stood a table – an upside-down pyramid of solid oak balanced on a triangular plinth – with three figures, two men and one woman clothed in sharp white, sitting on high backed chairs placed around it. In front of this set in the floor was a mosaic made from different shades of marble, creating a trefoil – a shape made up of three circles.

"Welcome to our humble abode," sneered the man sitting to Erin's right. His thick caramel hair curled to his shoulders, and as he spoke, he fingered his rough, straggly beard. "We hope you had a pleasant journey."

Erin swallowed hard. This was Trefoil. The three people who made all the decisions. The woman to her left was Joyce Williams, whom she had met at the fireworks factory. Joyce's face was like porcelain, her icy blue eyes sparkling in the light, while reams of silver-blonde hair were draped artfully above a high forehead. She turned her face to Erin. "It is very nice to see you again." Her voice was brittle.

"Enough of the chit-chat." The man sitting in the chair facing her now spoke. His educated voice boomed out. "I am Oliver Irons, the CEO of Pro-Di-To and director of Trefoil, our education division. Joyce Williams, you have met before. She is the director of Flame, and this is John Johnson, our director of Sail Away."

Erin now focused on Oliver Irons. He had a presence about him giving him an aura of authority. Eyes, the colour of walnuts, stared out from under neatly manicured eyebrows. His olive skin contrasted with the pale features of Williams, and his receding hairline was the antithesis of Johnson's shaggy mane.

"Why have you brought me here?" Erin uttered, coughing to clear her throat. "Where am I?"

"Always so many questions," Irons said. "This is our headquarters." He waved an arm to encompass their surroundings. "We are beneath an historical building known as Trefoil Lodge. You were held in one of the cells on the top floor."

Erin coughed again; the cold from last night had seeped into her chest.

"We decided it was time to talk with you," Irons continued. "As you have been told before, you and your sister are important to us – two of our chosen ones. It is time for you to understand why and what we require of you. We apologise for holding you in one of the top floor cells. It was necessary. Please sit down. You will find refreshment on the table, help yourself." Irons pointed to a chair next to a side table on which a jug of water, a glass and a plate of plain biscuits were laid.

Erin wasn't sure what she should do. Should she stand and rail at them or rest a while to gain some strength? The latter seemed the best option, so she sat down. Glugging back some water through parched lips and then downing some biscuits made her feel a little better, and she straightened her aching back and lifted her chin. I will listen and take my cue from them, she thought.

"Silas Winslow, a highly respected scientist and his wife, Joyce, an award-winning artist, were your grandparents." This was from Williams. Erin gasped. She wasn't expecting this. What did they have to do with all of this?

"Sadly, they were lost in a tragic accident. Both Silas and Joyce were part of NN2000. In the 1990s, before you were born, they worked alongside Trefoil and Pro-Di-To in building the foundations of our education department. If they were alive today, they would be sitting here with us."

Erin couldn't take it all in. My grandparents? Dad's parents were part of this corrupt regime? No, that can't be. She shook her head as though that would change anything. Did Dad know about this? Feeling light-headed, she bent forward and cradled her head into her two palms.

Williams paused and then resumed her explanation. "Yes, a chemist and an artist, just like Miranda and you. They would have been pleased with your participation in developing a work force Britain will be proud of. They would have been so proud of you both and your contribution in changing the course of history."

Erin lifted her head. "What do you mean? We have had no part in your cruel plans."

"Dear me, have you forgotten about the fireworks? Miranda's suggestions for the chemicals and your designs for the butterfly explosions. Oh, and we mustn't forget Frankie, must we?" Williams scoffed. "John will tell you more of what Frankie has been doing."

"Thank you, Joyce. Yes, Frankie has played a huge part in our boat designs at Sail Away." His gravelly voice grated on Erin. "We are based in Cornwall, and Frankie Mallory, along with his sister, Cara, have been working on the computers within our two fire boats." John Johnson smirked at this. "He even named the boats for us. As our operation for 5th November 2018 is called *Paper Boats and Butterflies*, he suggested we called one *Bateau de Papier*, and the other *Papillon*."

Rage twisted Erin's stomach. Frankie? How could he be working with them? Her mind was racing – computers, butterflies, paper boats, fire – what did they mean?

"What is a fire boat?" Erin asked, her voice husky with dread.

"You don't need to worry about those apart from the fact they will be transporting your fireworks across the River Thames for the celebrations."

"Celebrations?" echoed Erin. "What celebrations?"

John Johnson sprang to his feet; an imposing figure in a pearl-white Nehru jacket over matching trousers. He swept tangled curls back before dropping piercing eyes of steel to scrutinise Erin. "We are celebrating what my ancestor, John Johnson or as you know him, Guy Fawkes, set out to do back in 1605. We will finish what he and his fellow conspirators started, but not for the Catholics. This time for us at Pro-Di-To."

Erin's eyes flicked back and forth as her brain tried to decipher all that he was saying. Guy Fawkes? Somewhere in her mind, there was a link. Screwing her eyes up now, she tried to think. Why did the company name mean something? She shook her head. I can't remember. Another voice broke into her thoughts, forcing her to come back to the present.

"We have decided to do a rehearsal this year,"

Oliver Irons said. "We need to ensure nothing goes wrong this time. That is where you come in. You will be taken to London and will play a vital role in this."

"And if I don't do as you ask?" Erin said, realising that if she followed their instructions, she might be able to stop them.

Irons' expression shifted. Where his gaze had been almost paternal, it was now of hatred. Like storm clouds blocking out the sun, his eyes darkened, and the light within them vanished. "You will do as I ask because you are in debt to our company. We believe it was your father who caused the accident, leading to Silas and Joyce Winslow's death. If you or any of your so-called Teardrops do anything to prevent this from happening, Patrick Winslow will be tried for parricide and will be sent to prison never to see the light of day again."

Frankie: Further notes from Trefoil Tablet

Research by Silas Winslow.

Apparently, he gave advice to Trefoil in the 1990s. He seems to have done a lot in looking at chemical imbalances of the brain and how it can affect a person's character.

Some of his research was into experiments on the brain throughout history — lobotomies, electric shocks etc. From what I can see he wasn't condoning this form of treatment; he was investigating it because he was genuinely interested in the subject. His explorations led him to the use of therapy and care when treating a patient. Trefoil seem to have adapted the more macabre ideas for their schools.

Research by Professor Douglas Mallory

I have discovered my father was a descendant of a man who worked with the doctors in the concentration camps during the Second World War. I found copious notes referencing the experiments carried out. Again, just like Silas he was interested in learning from the mistakes of our ancestors. When my father, Professor Mallory, worked as an advisor for Trefoil, they were interested in his research; they twisted his suggestions to suit their own evil requirements. I have included some quotes from his work.

- 'Looking at psychiatric reports we have found if you separate twins at birth, it can allow them to develop at their own rate and form their own personality.
- Boarding schools can ensure parents do not affect the individuality of the child.
- Recent education reports have shown boys are not performing as well as girls. However, it is important we offer an equal education to both genders. It must be controlled and challenging.'

Chapter 10

"What do you want to do?" asked Nadir.

Miranda rubbed her hands through her hair and then, shaking her head, said, "I don't know. I'm so worried about Erin, I can't think straight. What will they do to her this time? We've been fighting against them all this time, and I think they may have won."

"It's not over 'till the fat lady sings."

"Which lady? I can't keep up with you, Nadir."

Nadir laughed, a warm rumbly laugh, and explained what he meant. Miranda sighed. "Okay, let's do something. We can't stay here for ever." Pressing her hands down onto the ground, she swivelled her legs round to kneel. "Hold on a minute. We could break the padlock. It's very corroded, so it might give way quite easily." She looked around her, searching for a rock, unfortunately the tunnel walls were smooth, and the ground clear of any debris.

"I'll have a go with my foot," announced Nadir.

He began to aim hard, fast kicks at the padlock. Nothing happened, apart from a loud jangling noise from the chain against the metal bars. Pausing to catch his breath, he leaned down and pulled hard at the chain. The padlock sprung open. "It wasn't properly locked after all that."

Miranda struggled to her feet. "You did it. That was amazing." Together they uncoiled the chain from the bars and carefully placed it on the ground. Nadir pushed at the door. It was stubborn to open and after Miranda added her weight it eventually succumbed, and they were able to enter the tiny cell. No doors or windows, just a rusting ladder bolted to a wall and shining her mobile torch up to the ceiling above, Miranda could make out a trapdoor.

"You first," urged Nadir.

Gingerly, Miranda placed her right foot on the first rung and pulled herself up. Checking each step before ascending, it took some time until her head finally grazed the trap door. Nadir shone his light upwards, and she soon made out a small circular handle. It turned. A click resonated, and before she knew what was happening, the trapdoor swung down towards her. Miranda ducked just in time, but Nadir wasn't quite as fortunate. Soil, weeds and gravel tumbled down through the small aperture and hit him squarely in the face.

"Sorry," whispered Miranda, looking down into the darkness below. "Are you all right?"

A spluttering and swearing informed Miranda he had survived the onslaught. Nadir's light came back on, his features a ghostly yellow. "No worries. Don't mind me. What's up there apart from all of this lot?"

Miranda resumed her climb and hauled herself out of the ground. It was night-time, and she fumbled with her phone to light the way. Mysterious white shapes materialised in the gloom and an enormous angel with broad wings reared up from nowhere. Miranda flinched as Nadir's grimy face popped out of the hole.

"I wasn't expecting that," he said, swinging his rucksack off his back and throwing it to the ground before heaving himself out to stand next to Miranda.

"Nor me." Miranda dusted herself down, brushing rust and mud from her clothes.

The trap door was within an enclosure constructed from granite strips, all smothered in moss and lichen. The angel statue, set on a stone plinth a few feet beyond the hole in the ground regarded them from on high, keeping watch over the churchyard. Nadir knelt quickly and pulled the door up until they heard the click and then covered it over with earth and gravel.

"I think I need a shower," he said. "Come on, we'll go to my uncle's shop. Then we can decide what to do."

Miranda nodded and followed him along the church path, through the open gates, along winding streets until they reached the grocery shop. Nadir rooted around in his jacket pocket and produced a set of keys. They were soon inside. The sound of gunshots and shouting, and horses neighing in fear, could be heard from the room above. Without turning on the lights, Nadir led Miranda up the stairs to the flat. They crept past the snoring lump stretched out in front of the TV that was Jim Colly. Clint Eastwood stared down at them from the screen, then lifted the poncho he was wearing to reveal a huge metal plate strapped to his chest covered with dents from bullets. Nadir shrugged his shoulders in an apology and then showed Miranda into a room stacked high with boxes and an old camp bed squashed between cartons of baked bean tins and bags of flour.

"It's not much, but it'll do for tonight." Nadir left the room while Miranda stood waiting, unsure what to do. The boy returned with a cushion and some blankets, which he placed on the camp bed.

"What about you?" whispered Miranda.

"I'll sleep on the floor in my uncle's room. I'm just going to wake him and get him to bed. See you in the morning." He checked his phone for the time. "Oh, it is the morning. 3.20. No wonder I'm tired. Night." With that, Nadir turned away and left the room, pulling the door closed behind him.

Miranda made up the bed as best she could, and slipping off her shoes, she snuggled down fully clothed. Her last thought before giving in to slumber was of Erin.

 After the meeting, Erin was escorted to another area within the underground complex of Trefoil Headquarters. A beige Administrator showed her into a room that couldn't have been more different from the triangular cell in the building above. It oozed luxury and comfort. Erin bit her lip as she stood on the threshold, deciding whether to enter or not. The Administrator gave a sad smile and beckoned her in. Erin entered, presented with a folder and then left alone. The door closed softly behind her, and she stood still, her eyes darting from right to left, taking the surroundings in, allowing her brain to make sense of it all. Trefoil was playing with her mind. Don't trust anyone, she said to herself. I must remain on guard at all times.

The room reminded her of a five-star hotel with a sumptuous bed draped with a red and gold quilt and topped with several cushions. The walls were a muted amber colour, while the carpet was like a sandy beach. One wall was dominated by a TV screen, another by landscapes painted in thick oil and textured with fabric and leaves. A third wall contained an open door through which Erin glimpsed a bathroom. Erin walked across the room and sank into an armchair, the folder still in her hand. Laying it on her lap and studying it properly for the first time, she recognised the same creamy mother of pearl as the cover of the Trefoil tablet stolen from Zephyr all those months ago. Shimmering in the light from the chandelier above brought her to contemplate its demise at the hands of Cara and Professor Mallory.

Sighing, Erin opened the folder. It was like a hotel information pack – menus, who to contact, how to use the TV. On one page, it explained there were clothing and shoes in the wardrobe, toiletries in the bathroom, everything she needed for her stay. Rising and placing the folder on a round table beside her, Erin strode to the wardrobe. She gasped when she saw the array of clothes and footwear – jeans, T-shirts, sweatshirts, Vans and DMs. Everything she loved to wear.

A movement to her right made her look across to see a girl dressed in similar clothes, but this one was dishevelled with dirt on her face, framed by black rat-tail hair. Erin rubbed her cheek, and the other girl did the same. *I'm going mad; that's me.* She stepped towards an ornate mirror set in the wall and peered at herself. *I think it's time to take a shower.*

Later, Erin felt more herself – clean and dressed in new clothes from the wardrobe – but her mind wouldn't settle. With a cup of coffee steaming on the side table, she hoisted herself onto the bed, arranged pillows and cushions behind her and pressed a button on the TV remote. The screen on the opposite wall flashed into an array of colour and sound. Trying different channels, she finally settled on one showing a film of Anne of Green Gables – her favourite book. This was a version she'd watched many times and usually made her feel at ease, but today in this strange environment, it didn't calm her. All the things she had been told by Trefoil continued whirring around her head. Erin switched off the TV, and it became black once again. Silence.

Cradling her coffee, she focused on what she had learned about her grandparents' death. Oliver Irons had said it was Dad who killed them. I will not believe that. He couldn't. He wouldn't, would he? Irons twists the truth to suit him and his organisation.

John Johnson – the alias used by Guy Fawkes. Remember, remember, the fifth of November. Gunpowder, treason and… That was it. Mr Steele, my boring old history teacher with his piggy eyes squinting behind those thick glasses, has his uses. He told us Proditio is Latin for treason or betrayal. In fact, I remember him making a joke, which was rare, about his medication bearing the name

Pro-Di-To and how he thought it ironic the company name being akin to treason.

The name for their company – they say it stands for *Progression, Direction, Together.* Their TV advert slammed into her mind with their stupid jingle and idiotic catchphrase. They had duped the nation all this time. What would old Steely say to that? Hiding behind a legitimate company that trades throughout the world… oh my god… does that mean that Trefoil do the same? Are they doing this in other countries too? Erin's gut clenched with this thought. They can't be. How can I stop this? Just one girl against all of them. One against the many.

Erin sipped her coffee, the heat comforting her, the caffeine waking her up. Disjointed conversations came to her now. Their last conversation with Frankie, Pandora and Edward – just before the storm; before the argument with… Miranda… I hope she's safe. Wherever she is. And the policeman and his daughter – they were supposed to meet. He'll think they're not interested. And Frankie had finally shown his true colours and betrayed them with Cara. Oh God, this is all such a mess.

Muffled voices came from outside the door. Erin froze, straining to hear. Laying her cup down, she scooted across and pressed an ear to the wood. It didn't help. The conversation was still indistinct. Tentatively, she tried the door handle. It's probably locked, she thought. The handle turned in her grasp, and incredibly the door opened rather more quickly than she had intended. Not expecting that to happen, Erin went to close the door again, but not before hearing a voice she knew calling her name. Whipping the door back, she peered out. Frankie and Cara were standing to her left further down the hallway, their heads craning towards her.

All the resentment and rage that had been cloaked deep within her now rose to the surface. Her hands tightened into fists, her eyes narrowed, and her breathing quickened. She was poised, ready to attack.

"Erin? Is that you?" Frankie called out, beginning to stride towards her. "Hi. How are you?"

Cara followed him, and soon they stood directly in front of Erin.

"Is that all you can say?" Erin fumed. "Traitors. Both of you. I knew we shouldn't trust either of you."

"You don't understand," Cara was saying. Erin ignored her, focusing her gaze on Frankie, the boy her sister loves, the boy she had begun to believe could help.

"I could say the same about you and Miranda. Designing and creating fireworks to blow up the Houses of Parliament. You're the traitors." Frankie adjusted his stance and was now glaring back at her.

"What? No! We didn't know. We were just on work experience from school." Erin glowered back at him. "You've been working on computer systems on the fire boats."

The air was electric. One touch could start an explosion.

"Can we come in? We can't talk out here," Cara urged. Erin shifted her eyes to look at the ice queen.

As an answer, Erin turned and walked back into her room and waited. Frankie entered, preceded by Cara, who glided in and sat on the armchair. Frankie started to search the room, looking under the bed, feeling around picture frames, checking the light switches.

"What are you looking for?" Erin grunted.

Frankie didn't answer. He disappeared into the bathroom, turned on all the taps, then returning switched on the TV, tuning it to a radio station playing music. Erin recognised the heavy beat of one of her dad's favourite songs, The Jam, '*Going Underground*' distracting her for a moment until Frankie finally threw himself into a chair. She scowled at him.

"They've probably bugged the rooms," Frankie explained, his voice harsh, his face rigid. "We need to take care. Do you want to sit down?"

Erin shook her head and remained standing.

"I'm all ears," mumbled Erin, folding her arms and resting her hips against a table holding coffee and tea making items and a basket bursting with fruit.

"I know you've never liked me," Cara said.

"That's the understatement of the year,"

snorted Erin. "After what you did to my dad, I'll never forgive you."

"That was unfortunate but had to be done," Cara replied.

"I don't have time for this," Erin muttered with gritted teeth. "You're poison, through and through. I hate you and your father."

"Your parents are just stupid. What did they expect from getting involved in Trefoil? A nice easy life?"

"You conned my brother into believing you loved him. You manipulated him and us."

Frankie held up his hands at this. "Hey, that's enough. Both of you. This isn't helping the cause, is it?"

"The cause? What's that?" Erin asked, unfolding her arms in one swift movement and punctuating her question with hands outstretched. She curled her lip before adding, "Don't tell me, you're our saviour, come to save the world." Sarcasm dripped from every word.

"We have to work together. We are the chosen – you, Miranda and me. We are the only ones who can stop them." Frankie rubbed his chin where reddish whiskers sprouted. "I know Cara has done stuff in the name of Trefoil, but she had to. Our mother died at the hands of them because of what she knew. Cara was forced to do what she did."

Erin knew their mother was dead because of Trefoil; Edward had told her this in Zephyr. She shook her head. None of this made any sense. "I don't understand; why did you lead us to Zephyr? Why did you help with the escape?"

Cara opened her mouth to speak, no words came forth. A violent rattling of the door handle diverted everyone's attention. Someone was trying to get in. Erin flew to the door and yanked it open with such force the person there fell headlong into the room.

A cry came from the figure as Erin grabbed it by the throat from behind. Arms flailed around, and squeaks of indignation poured out before Erin realised it was Miranda she was holding. Letting go, she whirled Miranda round to face her. "I'm so sorry," she pleaded, wrapping her arms around to hug her twin.

Miranda coughed into Erin's shoulder. "I should have known you'd do this."

Erin led her over to the end of the bed, where they sat holding each other. Frankie, meanwhile, had filled a glass with water from the bathroom and offered it to Miranda. She smiled bleakly at him. "Hello," she croaked.

In answer, he patted her shoulder awkwardly and then pulled up a chair. Frankie leaned his elbows on his knees, not taking his eyes from her.

"How did you get here?" Erin asked.

"I don't know. The last thing I remember was being bundled into a car. I woke up in a stone cell and was taken to see Trefoil. An Orderly left me in a bedroom just down the corridor and I thought I would see if you were here." Miranda rubbed her knee and then her forehead. "I should have taken more care, knowing you and your karate."

Erin apologised again. A guitar riff ripped into the room – The Clash – Erin noted absent-mindedly, and the lyrics reflected her own thoughts. Should we stay?

From the other side of the room, Cara muttered, "We don't have time for happy family gatherings."

Miranda recoiled at the voice and looked across to the young woman lounging in an armchair. "Frankie, why is she here?"

"We were just about to tell Erin before we were rudely interrupted," Cara threw back.

Frankie leaned against the hard upright back of his chair, frowned at his sister and waited. Cara exhaled crossing her jeans-clad legs and folding her arms defensively.

"When Cara first met your brother in Cornwall, she wanted to help him. Professor Mallory, my father, had worked for Trefoil in the past as an advisor. When our mother died, he set about trying to find out what really happened to her. They knew a bit about Zephyr, but they needed someone to infiltrate the school. Cara had seen you both at the hotel when you first saw Miranda. She followed you back to your parents' hotel and then followed Mal to the petrol station. She started talking to him and, of course, the rest, you know Erin."

"But she helped them capture us. She sat there smirking when Miranda and I were in the glass observation room, in Zephyr." Erin rose to her feet and lobbed accusations at Cara. "They rewarded you. You bought the car. You helped them."

"So did your mother. Stella was rewarded too – lots of big orders from London, I believe she said," Cara hissed back.

"Our father lost his job because of Trefoil," added Miranda. "I was there when he came home drunk. It was awful."

"That's what we're trying to explain to you," said Frankie. "Trefoil use people; they have the power to drop you or raise you, and their threat is always against the people you love."

"So, what happened when you shoved Dad and me into the room hidden behind your fridge?" Erin asked, still unhappy with all the things she was hearing.

"And me," added Frankie.

"We were trying to protect you," Cara explained. "Trefoil came and took my father and me to Trefoil HQ. They took my beautiful car back and threatened us both. Then when we arrived at the house in Shropshire, we had to look like we were attacking Patrick…"

Miranda interjected, her voice rising in frustration. "The fire. You set the house on fire. People could have been killed."

"You sent your henchman to the swimming

pool to look for us," Erin declared.

"I thought you might have hidden in there. That's why I told them to come away." Cara pulled at her spiky hair. "Once you'd gone, we took everyone to the Terra school under the Wrekin. Everyone was safe. I apologised to your dad. Thankfully, I'm not very strong and quite a good actress."

"Where's Professor Mallory now?" Miranda asked, healthy colour returning to her cheeks, her forehead still a fierce red from the fall.

"Dad? He's working with Trefoil of course," Cara said, shrugging her shoulders.

"What? You can't be serious?" Erin shrieked.

"We're all working for Trefoil, for Pro-Di-To. It's the only way we can stop them. My father has the tablet from Zephyr and with the three memory sticks he and I have been able to piece together…"

"You gave him the memory sticks?" Miranda cried out.

Frankie's voice cut through the air and in the stillness that followed, he rose to his feet and strode over to Miranda. Gently taking both her arms, his final words poured balm onto the fire of her pain. "You have to trust me on this. We need you. We can't do this without you and Erin. Please…"

Miranda gazed back at Frankie and, turning her head, looked across at Erin for a sign. A slow nod told her that this was something they had to do.

"I trust you, Frankie. I always have," Miranda murmured.

Erin said, "All right. We're with you. I'm not going to pretend I like Cara, but I will work with her and you."

Cara muttered an agreement. "The feeling's mutual. Just don't attack me. Save your energy for the real work."

"Right," said Frankie. "Let's get down to it." He pulled a chair up to the table next to Cara. Miranda moved to sit on the side of the bed nearest to them while Erin remained standing.

Frankie resumed. "Cara and I have been working on the computer systems on the fire boats. I was sent to Sail Away to do work experience, just like you were sent to Flame Fireworks. I was introduced to John Johnson while there. They are subsidiary companies of Pro-Di-To. However, unknown to them, we've introduced a virus that will be undetected until the day of the operation. This is set to take them off course and away from their target."

"They told me they were carrying out a practice run this coming November," Erin remarked.

"Yes, that's right. The actual thing is set for 2018 when everyone in the four schools turn eighteen. They plan to insert the students into government offices and major companies that organise transport, finance and so on. Thought Reform will get them following Trefoil's instructions."

The song, *'We don't need no education'* filtered into the room, accompanying Frankie's speech.

"Why haven't they done that to us three?" demanded Miranda. "Surely, we would be the first ones they want to control. They've had so many chances to return us back to Zephyr and to mess with our brains."

It was Cara who answered. "We don't know. Frankie and I have talked this through with Amber Hessonite, Pandora, Edward and my father. Nobody seems to know why you three have been left to your own devices."

A sudden thought struck Erin, and she gasped.

"What is it?" Miranda asked.

"What if they've already done something to our brains? They carried out brain scans and all sorts of experiments on us all. How would we know?" Erin was still loath to trust Cara fully. Pinching the skin on her own wrist caused her to cry out. "That's good, I can still feel pain."

"It's not like being in a dream, Erin," Frankie said. "You can't just pinch yourself and know what is real and what's fake."

"We need to go down to Cornwall and see Dad and Amber," Cara announced. "They will know. They can check on you all. Professor Hessonite has worked in Zephyr from the beginning."

"How can we do that? We're stuck in here," Erin and Miranda chorused.

"Like we said, we have to do as Trefoil ask. I

believe there's going to be a meeting here tomorrow with the heads of the four schools. We've been invited to attend and swear allegiance."

Erin narrowed her eyes. "Why didn't you tell us this before?"

"Because you wouldn't let me explain. Anyway, I'm going to bed. Sleep well everyone. See you in the morning." Cara rose from her chair and drifted out of the room accompanied by the strains of another song from the 80s, this time a love song.

Erin looked across at the other two and realised Frankie and Miranda were gazing at each other. Clearing her throat she muttered, "I'm just off to the loo." On her return, she found the two of them now standing close together, holding hands. Erin coughed again, and like a spell being broken, they pulled apart.

"I'm off to bed," said Frankie, his voice suddenly hoarse.

"I'll come with you," added Miranda and then went very pink. "I don't mean… I mean…"

Erin laughed and shooed them both out. "Whatever," she said, closing the door firmly behind them. She felt a weight dropping from her shoulders. Finally, they've found each other.

Bowrider ⌄ Cabin Cruiser ⌄ Centre Console ⌄ Motor Yacht ⌄ Sedan Bridge

Open Days 📅

Here at Sail Away we take great pride in continuing the heritage of boat building in Petrock, Cornwall. We are passionate about our designs – both traditional and modern.

Our craftsmen will bring your dream to reality. By using the finest materials, we will fully equip your motor yacht with precision, perfection and promise.

When you purchase one of our sleek custom-made boats you will be able to *sail away* to wherever you want to go.

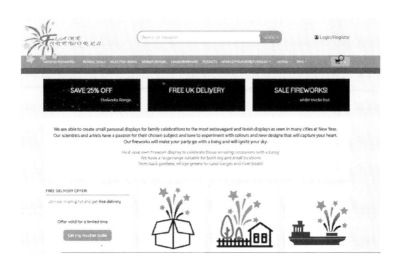

Login/Register

SAVE 25% OFF
Fireworks Range

FREE UK DELIVERY

SALE FIREWORKS!
whilst stocks last

We are able to create small personal displays for family celebrations to the most extravagant and lavish displays as seen in many cities at New Year. Our scientists and artists have a passion for their chosen subject and love to experiment with colours and new designs that will capture your heart. Our fireworks will make your party go with a bang and will ignite your sky.

Host your own firework display to celebrate those amazing occasions with a bang!
We have a huge range suitable for both big and small locations.
From back gardens, village greens to canal barges and river boats!

FREE DELIVERY OFFER

Join our mailing list and get free delivery

Offer valid for a limited time

Get my voucher code

Chapter 11

Miranda followed Frankie into the hallway. A warm fuzzy feeling was creeping around her body, and she didn't know what to do about it. Frankie took her hand and guided her to the door of her room, which he opened. Then he gently turned her towards him and whispered, "I've missed you so much."

She began to say how she had missed him too but before she could finish, his mouth was on hers. For a second or two, she drew back. This was something she had never experienced, and then when he tenderly stroked her hair, she softened, leaning into him. It was a gentle coffee kiss, sweet like caramel. Frankie pulled away, leaving Miranda with her eyes tightly closed. She smiled, opened her eyes and swallowed.

"Sorry," Frankie said, his voice hushed. "I should've asked."

"No, it's okay." A sudden heat struck her face, and Miranda glanced away from his piercing stare.

"I think I love you, Miranda. I'm not very good

with all of this. Zephyr gave us an abnormal idea of love. I just know I want to make you happy and protect you. Does that make sense?"

Peeping up at him, the boy with the red hair who she had missed every day since leaving Zephyr, she nodded. "I feel the same." She kissed him, savouring it properly this time. This time it was Miranda who drew apart.

"Good night," Frankie murmured. "See you in the morning." He strode off down the hall to his own room. Miranda watched him go and then went into her room and turned on the light.

The next morning, a sharp rap on her door awoke her. An Orderly pushed open the door and told her breakfast was being served in the main dining room in half an hour. After quickly showering and dressing in colourful clothes she found in the wardrobe, Miranda sat on a chair facing a dressing table and mirror. There was a glow in her face she had not seen before, and she smiled, thinking of Frankie and their two kisses. She combed her hair before reaching for her shoes placed neatly by the side of the chair.

Pulling the door closed behind her, Miranda set off towards the dining room. She was soon joined by Erin, and they walked arm in arm along the hallway. "This feels very normal and not normal at the same time," she whispered.

"I know what you mean," Erin replied. "Just remember to listen carefully to everything that is said today and keep your wits about you."

"You too," Miranda said as they entered a light-filled room with a large oval table in the centre and breakfast items laid out on a side table. There were no windows as they were underground. Light streamed down from millions of tiny bulbs spiralling from a high ceiling. Frankie and Cara were already seated and tucking into cooked breakfasts. Frankie glanced up at Miranda.

"Good morning," he said, grinning.

Something ignited within Miranda and a warmth coursed through her veins. Dropping her gaze to hide her desire to feel once again his lips on hers, she stopped still. What do I do? I don't know what to do.

Thankfully, Erin steered her away as though sensing Miranda's discomfort. "Come on you. I think you need sustenance." Erin guided her across to the table piled high with cereal packets, brown and white bread, fresh fruit, yoghurts, Danish and French pastries and rectangular metal dishes. On lifting the lids one after the other, the girls discovered they contained bacon, sausage and beans.

"Can I help you?" said a voice. It was an Orderly standing to attention at the end of the table. "Tea? Coffee? Hot chocolate?"

Miranda remembered the time when she first came home from Zephyr, and her mother bombarded her with similar questions. This time, however, she knew exactly what she wanted. "Hot chocolate and croissants please."

"Please take a seat, and I will bring it over to you."
The Orderly was incredibly polite, and Miranda
marvelled at his next words said to Erin. "And for
you, madam. How may I be of service to you?"

"The full works for me and a latte please."

The girls took their seats on the opposite side
to Frankie and Cara. Cara glanced up, her teacup
poised and said, "I trust you slept well."

Both Erin and Miranda grunted an
acknowledgement before helping themselves to
orange juice set out on the table. "This is like a
hotel," Erin stated. "In fact, it's better than a hotel
as we don't have to pay."

"Don't we?" murmured Cara. "Perhaps not
with cash, but we will have to pay in other ways."

This stultified any further discussion. The food
duly arrived and was placed in front of the girls.
They all ate in silence.

While she ate, Miranda reflected on how she
had finished up here after being with Nadir in the
tunnels hidden deep below Newton.

She had slept surprisingly well on the little
camp-bed squashed between boxes full of tins of
food. Nadir and his uncle Jim were very kind and
tried to put her at ease. Jim was astonished to hear
his suspicions had been correct, and he was ready
to tell the whole town on social media. Nadir
stopped him just in time before he could add
anything to the Newton notice board, urging him
to wait for a while until they knew they were safe.

Deep in her heart, she knew they were all in danger, and she didn't know what to do about it.

One thing she did know was they were due to meet with Sergeant Marston and Imogen at 10.15 that morning. Texting Petra to ask her to come along too and the immediate reply of a purple heart and a YES in capital letters boosted her confidence. She wasn't alone.

Nadir had accompanied her to the coffee shop where the policeman and a girl with a heart shaped face and a mass of frizzy curls, were already ordering drinks. Sergeant Marston insisted on paying for them and Petra when she eventually showed up. They all squeezed around a table, everyone introducing themselves before diving into the plate of cakes Sergeant Marston had ordered. Miranda was starving, having only a mouthful of chocolate and some biscuits since yesterday's lunch at home with Erin. Erin… where have they taken her? She pushed down the growing anxiety of her sister's safety and listened to the discussion.

Sergeant Marston explained to them he had worked in London and York as a young constable. He still had friends in the Metropolitan Police, and he told them he could call in some favours. Imogen had some suggestions too – she was keen to help in any way she could. Unlike her father she spoke softly with no hint of an Irish accent and was slight in build. The emerald green of the eyes was the only thing they shared. That and a love of cake!

After leaving the café and saying goodbye to the Marstons they had returned to Jim's flat where Miranda and Nadir, along with Petra, began to make plans.

It had been around three in the afternoon when Patrick suddenly appeared in the flat.

He wasn't alone.

Two muscle-bound Orderlies trailed after him. Jim was working downstairs in the shop; Petra had returned home, and Nadir had gone out for provisions to cook dinner. Alone and helpless against the strength of two men she found herself being dragged down the stairs, through the empty shop – Jim Colly was nowhere to be seen - and shoved unceremoniously into the back of a car. Throughout this, her father had called out to her, apologising and admonishing the Orderlies for the way they were manhandling his daughter. Before the car door slammed shut, her last view was of Patrick with anguish painted across his face, stretching out his hands, entreating her to forgive him. One of the Orderlies blocked her vision, plunged a needle into her arm, and then everything stopped for Miranda.

Now, as she finished her breakfast, her mind was made up. She needed to know the truth. She wanted to end all of this pain and distrust once and for all.

At 11am sharp, they were summoned to The Sanctum. The Chosen ones were led by an

Administrator dressed in a beige suit and shown three chairs set out for them. Each chair had a side table with glasses of water ready, plus notebooks and pens. Cara was asked to sit away from them, and she complied politely.

Four people, all dressed in purple, came into the room and took their seats. The four principals of the schools passed by, glancing briefly at Miranda, Erin and Frankie.

"All rise." The instruction came from the Administrator, and everyone stood. The three members of Trefoil swept in, all in pure white and took their places at the triangular wooden prism which seemed to hover above its plinth.

"Welcome to you all," Oliver Irons boomed out. "Please sit."

Miranda took her seat just like everyone else and waited, her hands placed in her lap, her knees pressed close together.

"Our first time of being together as one. This is a special day." Irons' plummy, educated voice echoed around the room. "Today we welcome The Chosen – Erin and Miranda Winslow and Franklyn Mallory. We should have had a fourth here today, but circumstances beyond even our control mean that George Mallory is lost to us. However, Cara Mallory is with us, and she will play her part."

Erin glanced across at Cara; a ghost of a smile came to her scarlet lips. What does she really think? thought Erin. Can I finally trust her? Erin concentrated on breathing. The in-breath and the out-breath. I must be aware of all things. I must practise Zanshin just as my karate instructor has taught me. I must stay calm and listen carefully.

She took the spiral-bound notebook and pen from her side table, noticing for the first time the front cover bore an image of a skull, the left side bearing a metal plate in contrast to the right side, smothered with flowers growing from a huge crack in the bone. The skull hovered above water where a paper boat floated. Erin's eyes were drawn towards the left eye socket – a patch of blue – a tiny butterfly beating its wings against a bony cell.

As an artist, she appreciated the beauty of the image and having experienced Zephyr first-hand, she saw nature and nurture being expressed so clearly. A voice she recognised and dreaded broke into her thoughts, and she realised her Zanshin had escaped her for her love of art. Esme Dorling, the principal of Zephyr, was speaking. Erin folded back the cover of the notebook and raised her eyes. Miss Dorling was standing, introducing the other three principals to them.

"This is Ian Adare of Terra and David Core of Ignis." The two men, both clean-shaven, one dark-skinned and handsome, the other a sickly-looking man, his skin pale and insipid. "Angela De Vate of Aqua. Of course, you know her already, your aunt, I believe."

Erin smiled inwardly as she looked at Miss Dorling's face – it hadn't healed well. The scars from the explosion of shards of glass, caused by the intrepid Edward, stood out like pathways on a map. She caught the principal's eyes boring into her, and she stared right back, willing the woman to react. Turning on sharp heels, Miss Dorling sat back down, crossed one leg over the other and entwined her fingers.

"Thank you, Miss Dorling. Now to business." Irons pressed his finger against the side of the table, and a screen came to life behind him. Simultaneously, the main lights dimmed, and the circles of the trefoil shape set in the floor began to spin around and lower down into the ground. A circular platform then rose up from within, revealing a 3D map. It remained unilluminated, waiting in the shadows.

"As you can see on the screen, two people who played an important part in building the foundations of Trefoil – Silas and Joyce Winslow… your grandparents…"

Erin and Miranda gasped in unison.

"…they were also taken from us. Patrick, their son, set off fireworks to celebrate the new year of 2005 and caused an avalanche that claimed our two founders. As you know, Silas worked alongside our team in the 1990s and was a strong advocate for our educational innovations. He was fully behind us in our quest to change this country. Joyce was his right-hand woman, of course. Her artistic talents can be seen in our logos and designs." At this, Erin turned back the cover of her notebook and saw JW hidden within the flowers covering the skull. Erin's skin prickled. *There is beauty and artistry here, and it is built on lies and evil.*

Looking back at the screen, as the image changed, she took a sharp intake of breath when she saw herself as a toddler holding hands with her grandmother as they posed for the camera in an enormous glasshouse. *What is that on my coat?* Erin brought her hand to her mouth and bit her nails – there on her shoulder, a luminous sky-blue butterfly rested while another danced on the tiny, opened palm of little Erin.

The image changed to a younger version of Silas Winslow – a teenage Patrick standing at his side watching his father fold a… paper boat. Erin didn't need to look at Miranda to see her reaction to this – the same pain stabbed at her own heart.

The screen changed again, this time showing their mum and dad dressed in their finery – going to a charity ball. Erin remembered the sketch she did of her mother when she had been imprisoned within Zephyr. It brought a glow to her heart to see that her pencil drawing was a good likeness – she had captured Stella's beauty as well as the sadness. Her father, dressed in a white tuxedo and black bow tie, beamed into the camera.

Irons was still speaking. "Patrick and Stella have helped us in many ways over the years. Their fighting spirit is reflected in their twin girls, Erin and Miranda. The girls have demonstrated nature and nurture throughout their lives. We knew they were intelligent and talented, but it is only since they turned fifteen that we have come to realise their true strengths. Infiltrating Zephyr, causing an escape…" His voice continued while a shard of ice slipped down Erin's spine.

"…of course, they have done all this without us knowing. And this is the most remarkable achievement. They are good at deception."

Erin swallowed her fear deep down inside her. His words 'without us knowing' echoing in her ears. She could almost feel the connections being made in her brain. They didn't know. Have they found out about our rave and being in contact with the other twins? I hope not. Erin mentally crossed her fingers.

The image on the screen changed and displayed an image of two people. One she recognised as being a young Professor Mallory dressed in true flamboyant style – red corduroy trousers, a purple velvet jacket and a bright yellow cravat at his neck. The woman she didn't know but assumed it was Frankie and Cara's mother. Her copper-coloured hair, the same as Frankie's, was scraped back into a ponytail. She, in contrast to her husband, wore black. No jewellery adorned her. There was no need as her stark beauty shone.

"We are indebted to Professor Mallory, Franklyn and Cara's father, for his expertise in both psychology and the sciences. Being a descendant from Heinrich Stein, who worked in the concentration camps, he has continued investigating how the mind and body work. Jessica Mallory sadly lost her life in a tragic accident." He tailed off to stare directly at Frankie. Erin saw the young man flinch.

She turned back as Irons continued. "So, we have our chosen ones. The offspring of our special people. They have all finally come to realise the opportunity we are offering them will continue what their ancestors began."

An image of two boats appeared on the screen.

"I will ask John Johnson to address you, now." Oliver Irons sank down onto his seat and helped himself to a sip of water before folding his arms. The sleeve of his jacket slid up, displaying a tattoo of a flame. Erin glared at the image. Fire – always fire.

John Johnson now rose to his feet. "These are the best we have ever created at Sail Away. I am delighted to introduce *Bateau de Papier* and *Papillon*. Our own paper boat and butterfly. Students from Zephyr and Franklyn and Cara have done a fantastic job of developing the structure to be fire-proof and impervious to bullets. The computer systems are second to none and are protected by several forms of security, so they cannot be tampered with by anyone."

While he spoke, a film showing every angle of the two boats unfolded on the screen. It finished with a close up of the names painted on the prow of each boat. *Bateau de Papier* was intertwined with illustrations of paper boats on an azure sea blending into the paintwork, while *Papillon* was dotted with butterflies of every hue. Erin recognised the images as some she had produced while working at Flame Fireworks. She tightened both hands into fists. Yet more of her artwork tied up with destruction.

Johnson pressed his finger against the side of the table, and a bright circle of light shone down from above, displaying the 3D relief map set out on the platform. He came forward carrying a remote control. "This will give you an idea of our final plans for *Paper Boats and Butterflies* for November 2018. However, as we said before, we will be carrying out a practice run this year." As he spoke, he operated the remote and different parts of the map lit up. "The London Eye on the South Bank will be where we will be positioned. We have arranged for the students from our schools to attend. They will be stationed in the pods and will be safe there. Our two beautiful boats will be moored at the Waterloo Pier."

Lighting up another area on the map, Erin could make out Big Ben and the Houses of Parliament on the other side of the Thames with Westminster Bridge spanning the river. Johnson resumed his talk. "We have decided to bring this year's operation forward to 16th October. The anniversary of the burning of parliament."

Erin stared at him. Burning? When was this?

As though reading her mind, Johnson explained. "In 1834, the buildings went up in a glorious fire. No misdemeanour then, just a good old-fashioned mistake. Burning the old wooden tally sticks in the two furnaces in the cellar. We feel this is a great anniversary to try out our boats. Finish off what Guy Fawkes and his co-conspirators started in 1605."

Erin began to calculate the time they had left. April until October – a matter of five or six months.

"I believe Joyce Williams has something to share with you now." John Johnson had returned to the side of the pyramid table whilst talking and now took his seat.

The woman in white now rose. The slide show moved on to images of the fireworks – in their new packaging designed by Erin, and then to images and recordings of them lighting up a night sky. The butterfly shape could be seen clearly against the inky darkness. She described the tests they had conducted and how there were some faults still to be sorted out. Williams finished by saying that Miranda had suggested some very new ideas in combining the chemicals, and they were indebted to her for her expertise.

Erin sighed as Williams sat down. She looked down at the open notebook – covered in doodles – she had not written anything useful. I just hope the others have written copious notes. She took a side glance without moving her head to look at Miranda's notebook. She was several pages in, her neat handwriting set out on every line. Erin glanced back to Frankie's notebook. His was still on his side table. Not even looked at. I hope he can use his photographic mind for this stuff, thought Erin.

During this time, Oliver Irons had been speaking to Principal Dorling, but Erin had missed it. The first thing she took in was a name – 'Amber Hessonite' and then the word 'education' and 'express request'. She sat up, straining to hear what else was being said. Miss Dorling was nodding and then looked across at the three of them. What have I missed? Me and my concentration. Just like school.

Suddenly, everyone stood up and filed out, leaving the three of them and Cara. Erin hissed to Miranda, "What just happened? I didn't hear the last bit. What was that about Amber?"

Miranda looked back at Erin and smiled. "They said we are to remain here until the practice run in October, and Amber has requested to come and complete our education while we're here."

"Do you think that's a good thing or a bad thing?" Erin whispered.

"Let's wait and see."

Trefoil HQ Presentation

Miranda Winslow

<u>Notes on River Thames Celebrations</u>

Taking place on 16th October 2016 — London will be
celebrating the history of London and the River Thames.
Frankie, Erin, Cara and I will be presenting our section of the river from
Westminster Bridge.
We will be seen on television by millions.
I need to research the history of The Houses of Parliament,
Big Ben and The Gunpowder Plot.
Look into the fire at H of P.
We will be staying in a hotel near The London Eye. This will be our base for the
weekend of the celebrations.

<u>General thoughts</u>

- Check details of what happened in The Alps in 2005 avalanche,
  how many dead, who was there?
- What was the role of our grandparents in all this?
- We are The Chosen Ones. What have they planned
  for us? Will we survive?

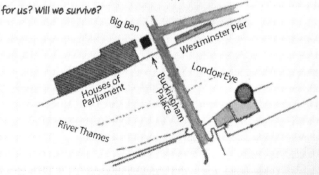

Chapter 12

 The room they were shown into was like a standard classroom – rectangular wooden desks set out, each with its own computer. The room was carpeted, which softened any sound of their feet as they entered. A red swivel chair was arranged in front of each screen where the Trefoil logo could be seen clearly. Amber Hessonite was already in situ; her orange outfit glowing like fire.

"Good afternoon, everyone. Please take a seat." Amber seemed distant to Miranda. This was a woman who had taught her in Zephyr and was seen as one of them, and yet she had been an ally all the time watching their backs, protecting them along with Edward. Good old Edward. She sat down, not sure what was going to happen. They had been told their education would continue here. Back home in Newton, they would have been sitting their exams. She had looked forward to that and was now pleased she might be able to take them. She waited while the others took their seats. Cara had joined them, even though Miranda knew she was nineteen and wouldn't be taking GCSEs. *What does she do for a job? She must have been working before all of this, but what? I've never thought to ask her, but then she's not the kind of person you can get close to.*

"Thank you," Amber said, looking towards the door, her face serious, her voice sharp and direct. Miranda spun round to see who she was talking to. It was an Orderly. "You won't be needed here. You can leave," Amber ordered.

"I have strict instructions to remain here," replied the Orderly, taking up a position by the door.

Professor Hessonite pulled herself up to her full five-foot one-inch height and, with her eyes blazing, yelled at him to leave. "I do not need a minder when I am teaching. Get out. NOW!" The final word came out as a shriek.

The Orderly backed out of the room, apologising, and pulled the door closed.

"Now, where were we? Ah yes. Good afternoon. It is wonderful to see you all again." Amber Hessonite was beaming. "Please bring your chairs up to my desk so we can talk properly."

The three girls promptly stood up and wheeled their chairs forward, while Frankie just rode his chair to the front with a big grin on his face. "Good to see you, Amber," he said, nearly colliding with her desk.

"It is wonderful to see you smiling, Frankie," replied Amber as she made several attempts to perch herself on the desk. Not quite reaching it, she leaned against it instead. "We are free to talk. I asked for all cameras and listening devices to be removed so they would not encumber our learning. Now, we have a lot to discuss."

Miranda felt cheated. She so wanted to improve her education and to have the chance to prove her intelligence through proper examinations. Her distress was obviously apparent to Amber as the woman enquired if she was unwell.

She nodded and then looked down at her hands in her lap. She had been wringing them without realising. Another hand came into view and grasped her two hands. It was her sister.

"She's okay, Amber. Miranda is disappointed she won't be studying for her GCSEs. Isn't that right?" Erin was smiling.

"Oh, don't worry about that, Miranda. We'll still be doing schoolwork, and you will be taking some exams," Amber explained.

Miranda sighed. "Thank you. That's great news."

Beside her, Erin snorted, letting go of Miranda's hands. "What? I thought we wouldn't have to. You're joking, aren't you?"

Amber shook her head. "No joke. Trefoil wish for you to be well-educated. Today, though we're going to start making plans."

A deep sigh came from Erin, and this time Miranda took her hand and squeezed it gently. "It's okay," she whispered. "I'll help you with chemistry."

The others laughed.

Amber brought them up to date on what she, Pandora and Edward had been doing. Miranda was amazed, and for the first time since being ensconced within the underground world of Trefoil, there was a glimmer of hope. Perhaps, they could stop them after all.

"I want to show you something," Amber said, pulling herself away from the desk and going round to her computer.

"Before I do, this is one of the most important discussions you will have. It is paramount that you listen carefully to what these people have to say and that you trust them implicitly. Without them, we will never be able to beat Trefoil."

The atmosphere in the classroom seemed to change. Miranda wondered who they would be talking to, and she sensed Erin and the others were thinking the same.

The screen behind Amber's desk showed a room. Miranda was confused. It looked like their dining room back in Newton. Then Stella appeared, followed quickly by Patrick. Their faces loomed large as they leaned towards the camera before sitting down.

"Can you hear us?" Patrick was saying.

Miranda held on to Erin's hand. Both girls were

still, unbreathing, biding their time.

"Loud and clear, Patrick," Amber replied.

"Thank goodness, you're safe," Stella said, bringing her face close to the camera and speaking loudly. Patrick could be heard telling her she didn't need to do that, just to be normal. In answer, Stella gave a sad smile and apologised. "You know me and technology. Not a clue."

"Mum… Dad…" Erin began, her voice petering out. She sniffed and used her free hand to rub her nose.

"We have a lot to tell you, to explain to you, but first…" Stella trailed off. She dabbed at her nose with a paper hankie. She continued, her voice thick with emotion. "Erin… I'm so sorry for all the pain I have caused you… I love you so much. The things I've done… I had to do. Can you find it in your heart to forgive me?"

A heartbeat. A needle dropping. Then, Erin spoke. "Mum, I'm sorry too. Of course, I forgive you. I love you. I love you both."

"And Miranda… can you forgive us for sending you away?" Stella asked.

"There's nothing to forgive… Ste… Mum," Miranda replied. "I know you did what was best at the time. You didn't know what was going on."

"Thank you," Stella whispered and bowed her head to wipe away tears.

"Are you being looked after?" asked Patrick.

"We're surprisingly comfortable," Miranda answered.

"Cara and Frankie – thank you for looking after our girls," Patrick said, his gaze turning to the other forgotten two.

"It was our pleasure, Patrick," Frankie answered. Cara said nothing and remained stony-faced.

"Dad?" Erin said, fear wrenching at her stomach. She had to know.

"Yes, my lovely girl. What is it?"

"Is it true? They're saying you killed your parents. Was it you? Was it an accident?"

Patrick removed his glasses and rubbed his face before replacing them. "It wasn't an accident."

Erin was aghast. "You murdered them?"

"No, no. It wasn't me. Let me explain." Patrick raised his palms imploring her to listen. "We were skiing in the Alps. You were only four or five at the time. You probably don't remember much about our holiday. My parents had decided to take the cable car to a different slope – a black run – they were experienced skiers. You and Mal were getting tired, so Mum took you both back to the hotel. I'd been chatting to a guest in the hotel who was organising the new year fireworks and agreed to help him with a problem with the computer he was using to set off the fireworks at timed intervals. Anyway, I wasn't in any way good enough for a black run, so I came back with you and went to see this bloke.

"It was an accident, or so I thought at the time. The fireworks' timing was all wrong. They went off too early while my mother and father were still out on the mountain. The people in the town said it was the worst avalanche they'd ever experienced." Patrick paused and took a sip of something from a mug and then resumed.

"The rescue team finally found their bodies a couple of days later. I wasn't blamed for it, and when the authorities went looking for the fireworks chap, he'd disappeared. He called himself Guy something or other – I remember thinking the irony. It was an awful time for all of us. The police tried to track him down, even Interpol was involved, but nothing came of it.

"I never saw the man again until I was taken to the Terra school at the Wrekin in Shropshire, you know, after the fire. There he was." Patrick took another sip of his drink. "Erin, do you remember when we saw Mum at Trefoil HQ, when we were studying the Zephyr tablet?"

"How could I forget it?" Erin murmured.

"You said something about a mark on the man's arm – a tattoo or something."

"Yes, it was a flame."

"I wasn't paying much attention; I was too wrapped up in finding Stella." As Patrick said this, he glanced at Stella. In answer, she smiled and stroked his face.

He continued with his account. "With everything going on after that, I forgot about it. We were taken to Terra School – a carbon copy of Zephyr inside – sterile and white, and that was where we met Oliver Irons for the first time. This was Guy from the fireworks incident. Ten years older, but it was him. He even showed me his tattoo when I questioned him."

Erin sat transfixed at the screen and then blurted out, "Are you saying Trefoil killed my grandparents?"

Patrick nodded. "Oliver Irons told us my parents had been involved in the setting up of the schools, how my father, Silas, had helped them and how my mother had produced artwork for them…"

At this, Erin stormed at her father. "How can your father, our grandfather, have become involved in the first place? How could our grandmother have allowed her artwork to be used?"

Patrick's eyes flickered for a second at Erin's salvo of accusations before resuming his explanation. "Once Mum and Dad discovered Trefoil's true purpose, they refused to continue working with them. My parents were good people with the very best of intentions. My mother's stunning artwork was a symbol of hope within the chaos of life. When she painted the series of skull pictures, she created them through love and then Trefoil stole them. Even worse my father's research on the brain was manipulated by these infernal people in the name of education. Mum and Dad threatened to expose Trefoil, and consequently they were eliminated from the project. Oliver Irons said he had proof that I had caused the accident, and he would go to the authorities with his evidence if I didn't cooperate. We had no choice."

Beside her, the tension building up inside Frankie was palpable. He suddenly erupted – a fountain of blame and accusations came pouring out.

"What? Why? Are you stupid or something? You adults make me sick. You think you can play around with young people's minds, sell your children. Didn't you ever put two and two together?"

Patrick and Stella looked downcast. "We're so sorry. We believed what we were doing was the right thing. Angela, Stella's sister, promised us everything would work out well for the children. She was a highly respected teacher, for God's sake." His soft, gentle voice rose in his frustration. "We trusted her."

Stella laid her hand on Patrick's arm to calm her husband. "Angela met Patrick's mum and dad at our wedding," Stella added. "Silas had suggested she apply for the role of principal at this new style school in Yorkshire. She got the job. We never knew she was working for Trefoil until she forced us to sell one of you. There have been lies at every turn, and now we want to make it right…"

Miranda suddenly interrupted their mother's flow. "What about your meetings with Miss Dorling and Angela De Vate?"

Stella's answer was to look from them to Patrick and back again. "How do you know about them?"

"I saw you," Miranda said blankly.

Cara intervened. "My father, Professor Mallory, has been working with both Stella and Patrick to clear their heads of the Thought Reform they might have experienced."

"Mum has continued to do the meetings; otherwise, Trefoil will suspect something has changed," Patrick explained.

"Patrick and I have been working closely with the others…" Stella began.

"Others?" echoed Miranda.

The screen abruptly changed to show a set of equations and formulae. "And that's why you need to take your time and concentrate on showing your working out," Amber said, raising her eyebrows.

Erin hadn't heard the door opening behind them. Twisting in her seat, she glimpsed the Orderly, the one from before, walking towards them. He was carrying a tray laden with mugs, a teapot, jug and a plate of cakes. The absurdity of this wasn't lost on Erin. She had just heard about her grandparents' death, and here they were being served chocolate brownies.

"Thank you, O9. We could do with a break from our algebraic equations." Amber gestured to the man to place the tray on one of the desks. He stood to attention.

"That will be all. You can go now." Amber was insistent. He turned on his heels and left the room.

The air was still for a second or two, and then everyone seemed to all breathe out at the same time. "Grab some cake. My favourite, so save a piece for me," Amber said.

Erin poured out the tea while everyone helped themselves to the food. In her mind, she kept going over the contradictions of this place, this company. One minute they were being thrown in a medieval cell; the next, they're having afternoon tea. They mess with your mind. They pick you up and drop you flat. Gazing around the room, she took in Miranda and Frankie standing close together. Frankie was gently wiping Miranda's face clean of chocolate. She was laughing as he murmured something to her. Erin was thankful that out of all this horrible mess, something good had emerged.

She glanced across to where Amber and Cara were in discussion. Talk about messing with your mind – Cara. What is she all about? I don't like her, never will. She's not a nice person, but I think she is finally telling us the truth. I will ask Dad if we get a chance to talk again.

"Right, everyone. Back to our maths," Amber announced. The door opened, and the Orderly appeared. He silently cleared away the plates and cups and then left the room.

"Can we go back to Mum and Dad?" asked Erin.

"Not today, I'm afraid. We really must do some maths," answered Amber in a clipped tone. "To your computers everyone."

Erin wheeled her chair to her desk. Ugh! I really don't want to be doing this. I suppose it will keep us occupied and will give me a chance to think over what we now know.

AVALANCHE IN ALPS   3rd January 2005

Worst in living memory!

On Friday, several avalanches struck the French Alps near the popular ski resort of Vald'Isere. It has been described as the worst for around 100 years, and yet incredibly, there were only two fatalities. Two very experienced British skiers were tragically killed; their bodies were found on 2nd January 2005. They have been named as Silas and Joyce Winslow.

Police believe a firework display set for midnight to celebrate the new year was accidentally set off early while skiers were still on the mountains. They would be interested in anyone with further information, particularly of a man known as Guy. Please contact the authorities if you can help.

Chapter 13

The next few months seemed to fly by for Miranda. They sat their exams, all three of them achieving high grades, Erin scraping a pass in chemistry and A* in art; they learned more about the plans for *Paper Boats and Butterflies*, carrying out further work on the boat designs and fireworks, being allowed out of the underground headquarters to visit Flame or Sail Away; they set up their own arrangements for the practice run and intertwined within all of this, Miranda and Frankie were becoming closer.

Over time, and bit by bit, Miranda and Erin gleaned information. Their friends, back home in Newton, had at first remonstrated with Patrick and Stella after the kidnapping. How could they do this again to their own flesh and blood? Mal along with Petra's parents brought the two factions together to become a joined force melding quickly and efficiently with the others.

Frankie suggested quite early on they take on the title he had invented whilst in Zephyr, and Erin and Miranda had readily agreed to it. The Teardrops made up quite a team on the outside. Miranda found herself looking forward to the conference video calls – she was someone they all respected and would look to for leadership at times. Alongside Erin and Frankie, and Cara, she was going to make a difference in their world.

Now sitting in the classroom gazing at the screen, Miranda thought about what would unfold in the next few days. It was now Friday 14th October. In two days, the world would learn of the evil plans of Trefoil and Joyce Williams, Oliver Irons and John Johnson would all be behind bars. Pro-Di-To would finally be exposed for what they really stood for, and Flame and Sail Away would be no more.

Miranda was dreading the next couple of days, yet deep in her heart, she knew the challenges they would face they would face together. The screen showed several squares, each containing faces. The Teardrops, formed from all generations, had laid the foundations by communicating with people across the country forming a superstructure, some of whom were to be stationed at vital points in London to ensure everything went smoothly. The four chosen ones were the keystone upon which everything depended; without them everything would collapse.

Her brother, Malachi, sat in one square, still in

York at his university. Another square held Pandora and Edward, and another, contained Elsie, Frankie's guardian. Miranda had wrongly assumed she was a frail grey-haired old lady and soon realised this was a woman to be reckoned with. Having worked at Bletchley Park towards the end of the second world war and being adept with technology, Elsie was an integral part of the secret plans. Elsie didn't trust Professor Mallory; she had worked with him years ago. Now, on the screen, they were shoulder to shoulder – in different houses, of course – and Miranda thought it ironic. It had been Elsie and her husband who had visited Frankie every five years, and now they were his guardians due to a request made by Jess Mallory in her will. They might not agree with each other's philosophy and might not even like each other, yet they were all in agreement that Trefoil and Pro-Di-To had to be stopped.

Professor Mallory, his usual flamboyant clothing a match for that of Elsie's vibrant paisley shirt and the flowery patterns of Pandora's top, could be seen in another square. Patrick and Stella, of course were on-screen within this chequerboard of faces. Another one held Rob, Nadir and Willow, and another held Neal, Bianca, Petra and Shay. The final two squares were people who had come late to the party, as it were, the police sergeant with his daughter, Imogen and three of the twins from the rave. Each one had a role to play in the bringing down of Pro-Di-To.

Erin went over the final arrangements for Sunday 16th October. "Don't forget this is a practice run for Trefoil, so the boats won't be carrying the fireworks. You all know where to be and at what time." Everyone nodded as one, except for Professor Mallory.

"Do you have a question?" Erin asked.

"Are you sure you know where the three of them will be stationed throughout all of this? We must ensure none of them escape," came a terse reply.

"Professor Mallory, we are as sure as we can be," Erin answered. Miranda could sense the tension building inside her twin and saw the automatic tightening of her right hand. It's all right, stay calm, Erin. Don't let him rile you. Miranda willed her sister to settle. She relaxed when she saw Erin's hand slacken.

"If there are no more questions then, thank you everyone, and good luck for Sunday," Erin said.

No one spoke. Everyone was still until a small movement came from Petra. Silently, she lifted her right hand, pressed the top of her thumb and forefinger together, her other fingers resting behind. One tear. Another movement – it was Nadir this time, and then Elsie did the same. As Miranda watched, each person on the screen raised their hands to form a teardrop. Drop by drop, the movement rippled, creating a whole sea of tears.

Miranda copied them, as did Cara, Amber, Frankie and finally Erin. Miranda glanced towards her sister, and when she saw her lift her left hand to form a mirror image of her right hand, she followed. The rippling on the screen became a wave, and as everyone brought their hands together, a kaleidoscope of butterflies hovered. United. A team. Together.

Erin nodded to Amber, and one by one, each square was closed. Leaving just Stella and Patrick. They each held up a paper boat; on the side of both was written the words WE LOVE YOU. Their square was then gone, and the screen's blackness seemed to fill Erin's head before she felt an arm slip around her shoulders.

"You were awesome," Miranda whispered.

"So were you."

Amber Hessonite stood up. "I think we should all get some rest. We have a big weekend ahead of us, and we need to be on the ball."

"What ball?" Miranda asked, moving away from Erin to stand and stretch.

Erin tutted. "Don't worry. There's no ball. We just need to be focused."

They all made their way out of the classroom and along the hall to their rooms. There they said their goodnights, and each one disappeared into their respective rooms.

Erin closed the door behind her and leaned

against the wood. This is it, she thought. Whatever happens, we have done our very best. This is our time to stand up to tyranny and treason.

Saturday morning came far too quickly for Erin. After a night full of dreams peppered with fire and explosions, she had woken early and stumbled into a hot shower to bring herself into the real world.

Breakfast was a sombre experience. Everyone ate in silence, occasionally looking at each other for reassurance that everything would work out.

Trefoil had arranged for the four chosen ones to be driven down to London to stay overnight in a hotel – a four-star near the London Eye. The three members of Trefoil were also travelling there by car and were to stay at one of the best hotels London had to offer, The Grosvenor House Hotel in Park Lane.

Erin, along with Miranda, Frankie and Cara, waited outside Trefoil HQ, marvelling at the three walls of the building above ground. Trefoil shapes and triangles were on every side, as windows and patterns. Two black limousines were parked on the narrow road, their drivers chatting, smoke billowing from their cigarettes. In turn the chosen ones placed their over-night bag beside the first car. Each containing a phone smuggled in by Amber – they needed to be in contact at all times. "Let's go." It was Amber Hessonite shepherding her flock into one of the cars. Erin remembered all those months ago, back in the summer of 2015, when she and Frankie escaped from Zephyr. It had been Amber then who had taken them to the hotel, but unbeknown to them at the time, she was an ally. Before she climbed into the car, Erin held back.

"Amber. I want to thank you for everything you've done for us. Not just for your teaching but for standing up to them." Erin hugged the woman standing in front of her – a vision in orange and amber.

It was an awkward embrace, and Amber pulled away, nodding and thanking Erin. "Come on, we must go," she said. Erin climbed into the car. A sea of darkness met her eyes. Each of the chosen wore matching suits as dark as pitch. She sat down next to Miranda, and Amber followed her in. It wasn't far to get to London – two and a half hours or so – and plenty of leather seating, a mini-bar, pillows and blankets would make their journey very comfortable.

Through the dim windows, Erin could see John Johnson, Oliver Irons and Joyce Williams, all dressed in their white suits, walking towards them and then they veered off at the gate to the second car.

The cars glided away, the outside world unaware of the occupants and their plans. Tomorrow, everyone will know the true meaning behind Pro-Di-To: treason, Erin mused. And tomorrow the truth will ignite the wrath of ordinary people. And tomorrow we will be free.

Early on Sunday, Erin found herself sitting in a coffee shop not far from the London Eye. It felt strangely normal. Everyone around them going about their business. People coming in and ordering food and drinks, some laughing and hugging friends, others looking tired and sad. She pondered on what their lives were like. Perhaps a nurse coming off duty or a retired teacher meeting up with old college friends. Of course, today was a special day for London, and it would be bursting at the seams soon, but for now, the café was still reasonably quiet.

Opposite her sat Frankie and Miranda, their hands entwined and Cara checking her bright red nails. Amber was alternately staring out of the window and checking her watch. Erin sipped her coffee, a latte and nibbled at a Danish pastry. She felt strangely calm. This was the biggest day of her life, and she sensed this would herald a new start, a new chapter. Yesterday afternoon, they had been taken to a huge office block in Canary Wharf, where Pro-Di-To was based; the company being the main sponsor for the extravaganza taking place on 16th October.

Whilst there, they were introduced to two people from the BBC who were going to present the show, Evelyn Starr and Larry Gibb, both well-known celebrities. Evelyn, a rather loud, quite brazen woman with white-blonde hair with darker roots showing through, greeted them with a cold hello. Larry, on the other hand, was much more amiable. He beamed warmly and shook their hands. An Administrator gestured for them to make themselves comfortable, help themselves to refreshments and to relax. The room with ceiling to floor windows was already quite full of people involved in the events. Erin and Miranda ambled across to a large map on the wall. They had only known about their section of the river and could now see the full scale of the celebration unfolded before them.

The title, *The Life Blood of London*, meandered across the wall above the map – pewter lettering outlined in blood-red. A spectacular event celebrating the River Thames, would be shown to millions all over the world. At the Tower of London, they were doing a re-enactment of the time of Henry the Eighth with boats transporting prisoners arriving at Traitor's Gate and at London Bridge, a film of the original structure housing many buildings would be superimposed on the whole bridge. It wasn't just going to be a celebration of historic events. The Royal Ballet would dance on the Millennium Bridge; the Tate Modern lit up with images of artwork and school children and adult choirs singing on many of the other bridges.

Erin pointed to the section of the Thames where they were going to be performing. Miranda studied it closely. Everything was set up. Everyone knew what they had to do. Nothing was going to stop them from unfolding the truth before the whole nation.

"Whatever happens tomorrow, we did our best," whispered Miranda.

"What if our best isn't good enough?" Erin sighed. "What if our plan doesn't work?"

"Well, we have to make it work, don't we?"

"Thank goodness they're not having the fireworks in the boats; they're just taking part in the flotilla of boats from all the ages. We can do our announcements quite safely. Trefoil will be high up in the top pod of the London Eye. They can't get to us down there on Westminster Bridge."

"Knowing that tomorrow people aren't in actual danger gives me the confidence to do this. It will just be about exposing Trefoil." Miranda gave a hopeful smile, and Erin returned one.

"The best thing will be seeing all the students from the four schools," Erin added.

Before Miranda could comment, Cara tapped Erin on her shoulder and indicated the buffet set out on a long table, where Frankie was already piling up his plate. "We'll talk later," said Miranda wandering across to Frankie.

Now, sitting in the coffee shop, Erin drained her cup and went to stand. She needed the loo. A sudden commotion at the door made her pause. Patrick was on the threshold, while three other familiar figures could be seen right behind him. For a second, Erin forgot to breathe. They weren't supposed to meet yet.

Patrick, along with Stella, Neal and Bianca, Petra's parents, wended their way through the many tables until they stood in front of Erin and the others.

"They've changed their plan," Patrick blurted out before anyone could say hello.

"Who's they?" asked Erin. A sense of foreboding washing over her.

"Trefoil are going to attack today," Neal interrupted. "Amber's just texted."

"What? Why didn't she text me?" Erin protested. Grabbing her phone, she checked, and there it was.

Fire Boats will ignite today.

Erin silently cursed not checking her phone. She hadn't heard it ping with the swelling noise of the café around her. Her heart hammered against her ribs, and she took a deep breath.

"We will follow the plan as before. Sergeant Marston has reported that he has spoken to several of the Met, and they will be positioned ready. This will really show the world what Trefoil are planning. We have to allow things to begin to happen so that we can show them in their true colours."

"That makes sense," agreed Patrick, rubbing a

hand over his bearded chin. "We'll get over to our places. See you later." Erin and Miranda hugged Patrick and then Stella in turn before they left.

"Good luck, everyone," Neal and Bianca said in unison and followed them out.

Erin turned back to the others. "First things first, I'm off to the loo. I'm desperate."

They remained where they were for a couple of hours longer. Each of them in their own little worlds. Erin checked her phone for the umpteenth time. Nadir and Petra had sent various messages of support. Finally, the time came. It was now or never.

Erin stood. "Are you ready?"

"Ready as we'll ever be," said Frankie.

They left the coffee shop and made their way out to the park near the London Eye. Several coaches were pulling up and disgorging their occupants. Students from Zephyr, Aqua, Terra and Ignis all dressed in dark blue with full heads of hair. They could be seen waiting while the teachers checked them. A memory came to Erin of a school trip here when she was in Year 7. Today was different from that time and yet very much the same. These students had all visited London via the Illusion/Delusion (ID) headset whilst being held underground. Walking through streets and marvelling at the striking sights and sounds of the metropolis. Now they were going to see it from on high.

The teachers, dressed in their customary bright colours, led them in long caterpillar formations towards the kiosks at the base of the London Eye. Erin searched the sea of faces for Cassie, Petra's sister and for the Teardrops, but they were too far away for recognition.

Everyone was to be in place by 2pm. Erin checked the time on her phone – it was now 1pm. Time to go. The four of them trudged along past the Eye – the pods taking their passengers into the sky – only the students, over 400 of them, the teachers and the three members of Trefoil were going to be housed here for the event. Erin and Miranda paused to watch as a sleek black car purred along the concourse and parked parallel to the Kiosk. John Johnson was the first to alight closely followed by Joyce Williams and Oliver Irons. All dressed in immaculate, ivory-coloured outfits. They strode into the glass-topped shelter and disappeared.

"Come on," urged Frankie, who was ahead of them. Erin and Miranda jogged towards him and Cara. It wasn't long before they were in their designated places – a mini stage enclosed by a Perspex triangular roof, placed at the centre of Westminster Bridge. Fluffy microphones and tiny earbuds were given to each of them, and they spent a few minutes fitting them in place and hiding the wires and transmitter within their uniforms of leggings and tunics, each the colour of a moonless night. They took their places. They tested each mic in turn with a sound engineer. A makeup artist fussed over them, ensuring they were looking their best for the cameras. Frankie waved her away, refusing to have any makeup and Erin giving him a sidelong glance, smirked. She joked it would bring out his eyes, and he huffed in protest as the woman moved in again to powder his face.

Giant screens had been set up along the Thames so the crowds could see all of the different spectacles. One had been erected above the entrance to the aquarium just near the bridge. Erin could see Larry and Evelyn sitting on copper-coloured seats, surrounded by green ferns and orchids and housed within a glass bubble perched on the grass near to the Houses of Parliament. They were describing what was happening along the Thames. The camera went to another presenter outside the National Theatre and then showed various actors performing.

Erin glanced over to the Eye – it was slowly revolving, each pod carrying several students in dark blue; the jewel colours of the teachers' uniforms strung through forming a necklace and the diamond at the centre of it all was the pod containing three figures in glistening white. The wheel would stop when the pod carrying Trefoil was at the top.

She turned back. It was nearly their turn to

speak. She adjusted her earpiece and could hear a countdown. This was it. There was no going back now.

A fleet of boats of all shapes and sizes and ages had set off earlier in the day and now were coming parallel to the London Eye. The two boats from Sail Away joined them here as well as a selection of other boats crafted in the 21ˢᵗ Century. From her vantage point, Erin could see the letters *Papillon* and *Bateau de Papier* – Butterfly and Paper Boat – painted on the sides. Her own illustrations dotted around the lettering.

The faces of Cara, Frankie, Miranda and Erin appeared on the huge screen. Cara began speaking. She described the boats in detail, spoke about the shipbuilding business in the UK and mentioned various famous ships, including the Titanic. Then it was Frankie's turn. He explained the importance of Westminster Bridge and described its history. He explained the green colour represented the House of Commons while the Lambeth Bridge, the next one along, was red for the House of Lords.

As the boats glided under the bridge, Erin noticed for the first time the pattern in the green walls on either side of the road. Trefoils. Of course. The four of them turned to now face upstream.

Miranda began her speech. She gave some history about the Houses of Parliament and Big Ben. Then retold the story of Guy Fawkes.

Throughout her speech, a film was superimposed onto the walls, and the politicians could be seen standing on the terrace.

"In 1834, a fire began in the basement. It soon became out of control," Miranda announced. The film on the walls now showed artists' impressions of the fire. Many of the boats were continuing their voyage towards Lambeth Bridge, leaving just a few in their wake. "This was the last fire that engulfed the parliament buildings, but…" Miranda paused and took a deep breath. "Today, there will be another fire. Today Pro-Di-To, a company who you trust, who have sponsored today's events, will attempt to destroy democracy. The two boats down there – Papillon and Bateau de Papier – are full of special fireworks…"

"…they are set to ignite soon, so please make your way to safety now." Erin stared around her. No one was moving. The crowds of people lining the banks of the river thought this was part of the show. She spun around and stared up at the top pod of the Eye. The pods had begun to move.

She shouted into her mic and pointed at them. "Trefoil, the three people who have set this up, are up there. They have created schools where children are abused. They are brainwashing young people to take over this country. They plan to lead the country…"

"…Erin… look." Miranda was pulling at her to turn round. Far below them, the two sleek boats were turning, perfectly synchronised. Grey smoke began billowing out of hatches in each boat.

"Frankie, check the controls," Erin hissed.

In front of them was a control board. Frankie was hurriedly pressing buttons, trying to shut off the computer systems onboard the two boats. Cara, beside him, was throwing suggestions at him. "We made sure this would work. We should be able to override it. Why isn't it responding?"

"I don't know," Frankie snapped.

Meanwhile, sections of the boat were now opening, and millions of brightly coloured sparks shot out high into the sky and then rained down into the grey water.

People on the banks of the river cheered and clapped. "Please, everyone. You are all in danger. Please leave the area immediately." Erin's final words were punctuated by a loud whooshing sound emanating from the two boats, and rockets fired high into the sky. Erin couldn't look. People were going to be killed. They hadn't managed to stop it in time.

"Hey. It's okay." Miranda was shouting. Erin twisted round to see, expecting to see carnage below. Instead, sparkly butterflies were filling the air. They hadn't hit their target, they hadn't exploded into the walls of history, they were safe.

People were clapping and cheering. The four chosen ones stood watching the fireworks. Erin croaked, "How? How did that happen?"

Miranda whispered, "It's a good job I'm good at chemistry. We didn't make them strong enough. The ones Trefoil had tested before had the full amount of explosive. We showed how they would damage walls and entire buildings. But these, thanks to Anaya, and a little help from me, were just an example of your lovely designs."

She spun round to look back at the London Eye. All the pods were empty. How can that be? "Trefoil. Where are they? Where are all the students?" Erin yelled, pulling off her earpiece and jumping down from the stage. "Come on."

The other three followed suit, and soon, they were sprinting along the bridge and down the steps to the walkway leading to the Eye. Their journey was hampered at every turn by the hundreds of people milling around, and Erin soon lost sight of the others. Finally, she turned the corner near the Eye and stopped. There were people everywhere. Where were Trefoil and the students?

Trefoil Education Process

Embryonic Phase 2000-2005

On entering one of the Trefoil schools, babies will become part of the Embryonic Phase. Each child will be designated a certain upbringing – either loving or broken. Their file will be stamped to indicate this.

Each child will become part of a monthly contingent. Their number corresponds to the time of their birth. As Plato said, 'Numbers are the highest degree of knowledge.'

After one year, parents will be invited to meet their offspring. They will not disclose who they are. They are allowed to refer to the child with a chosen name or the number we have given them.

Each student will repeat the Trefoil motto every morning until they are released in 2018. We are one being. We belong here. We are loved.

Larval Phase 2006-2010

After five years each child will enter the Larval Phase. Education will commence. Every child is to follow our own special system.

On the fifth year of their birth, parents will be invited to meet their offspring. As before, they will not disclose who they are. They are allowed to refer to the child with a chosen name or the number we have given them. This will be repeated at every five-year interval.

Chrysalis Phase 2011-2015

In their tenth year, education will continue. Monitoring of each child and their sibling will be strictly monitored throughout. Particular focus will be on their specialist subject.

Metamorphosis phase 2015-2018

The process of Thought Reform will commence from their fifteenth year. This will incorporate electric shock treatment, brain drugs, subliminal messages through music and video. Propaganda will be shown each week alongside these. The shaving of heads will continue throughout the whole process from birth to eighteen years.

Chapter 14

 Miranda chased after Erin, Westminster Bridge itself was clear of pedestrians and vehicles and she made her way easily to the top of the stone steps leading down to the walkway along the river. A sudden change to the image on the huge screen, above the aquarium, brought her to an abrupt standstill. There was Larry and Evelyn in their bubble, and with them were Stella and Patrick, along with Neal and Bianca, Petra and Cassie's parents. They did it, she thought triumphantly. Their words floated out into the air. "Trefoil must be stopped." And "Our daughters have experienced their cruel form of education."

The two presenters sat with their mouths open, clearly astonished at this intrusion. Patrick continued explaining to the millions watching all over the world that a respectable company, Pro-Di-To were responsible for the planning of heinous crimes against the monarchy and the government. He described the education processes that Trefoil were following to brainwash and corrupt children. Then the screen blacked out.

Miranda jogged down the stone steps, where the walkway throbbed with people, some gawping at the screen above while others shouted accusations into the air. Merging easily within the spectators, she blew pent-up air from her lungs and started to wind her way towards the Eye.

A flash of colour to her right and a voice she recognised roared out across the river. She froze, as did the crowd and as one body they turned towards the image of a man in white. "We cannot express how disappointed we are at these allegations being thrown at us and our very highly respected organisations." It was John Johnson speaking. "We are entirely blameless in this. These four young people have been plotting this for a long time. They call themselves The Teardrops and have been planning to take over our government. We never realised the full extent of their plans until today. They are responsible for the designs of the boats and the fireworks. They alone have set this up today."

Miranda's blood ran cold; they were being used as scapegoats. They had been set up, and now no one would believe them – four teenagers against a huge organisation.

Anger and confusion surged amongst the crowd like tendrils of smoke. A rough voice suddenly shouted, "That's one of them. Get her!" People began to jostle her trying to grab her clothes. Miranda screamed as a woman scratched her face.

Before she could fight back, everything went dark. Someone had thrown a heavy coat over her, and she was being hauled through the crowd.

"Help me, please. Someone. Help me." Her cries went unheeded, and she tried to fight her attackers. I am not giving up that easily, she thought. "Get off me," she shouted, lashing out with her arms.

A voice very close to her left ear said her name, and she flinched. "Stop fighting. It's me, Roberto. We're getting you to safety." They stopped abruptly, and Miranda found herself being uncloaked.

The afternoon sun was blinding for a second or two, and Miranda blinked hard before she could focus first on Rob, then Nadir and finally Willow and Petra.

"Sorry about that," Rob said as he pushed an arm into his favourite leather coat. "We waited at the end of the bridge and saw what was happening."

"Thank you, I think," replied Miranda, catching her reflection in the glass door of the entrance to the Eye. An image of tousled hair, clothing all rumpled met her gaze. "Come on, we need to get after the others. Can you see Erin or Frankie?"

"We lost sight of them back there," Nadir said. "Hang on, what's going on over in the park?" Miranda's eyes followed his arm to his pointed finger and beyond.

The park, adjacent to the London Eye, had become a seething ocean of blue. The students from the four schools had flooded the park and were held back by a human dam of teachers. Their brightly coloured outfits of purple, orange, green and yellow alongside dozens of beige Administrators and brown Orderlies formed a rainbow effect. And in the centre of the sea of people were three upright figures in white. The police had appeared and were making their way over to try and break it up.

Miranda ran through the twisting turning melee of people and soon reached the edge. Erin, Frankie and Cara were already there. From the very centre of the blueness came a voice, amplified through a microphone. "These are our students. You can see they are well and healthy. They are intelligent, well-balanced human beings. We are proud of our schools, and we look forward to the day they will enter the world of work and make Britain great once again." Oliver Irons paused and then asked one of the students standing next to him to speak.

"We are very fortunate to have been educated by Trefoil. We are well looked after and have had the best education anyone could ever wish for." He passed the mic to a girl who echoed what he said. The mic went to several students in turn, each one with dead eyes.

"The wigs," hissed Miranda.

"What?" Erin hissed back.

"They need to remove their wigs, then people will see them for what they really are."

Before Miranda could say anything more, a chilling voice rippled across to where they stood. "It is the Teardrops who have been against the government all along. They are responsible." Miranda stared at the blank eyes of Z11, a Jancon student whom she remembered from Zephyr.

Oliver Irons intoned, "You are one being. You belong here. You are loved."

Miranda's body straightened, her head faced front, her arms clamped her sides. Then, her mind blanking, she repeated the chorus along with over 400 Trefoil students. "We are one being. We belong here. We are loved."

 Erin's heart stopped. The world seemed to stop. All the faces of the students, including her beautiful sister and Frankie, showed no expression. Dilated pupils held no emotion while these hated words poured from their lips.

Whispers began behind her.

People in the crowd were murmuring.

She had one chance left. She grabbed Nadir's hand and yelled to him and the others to follow her. "Wigs!" she shouted. "Take off their wigs."

She broke through the barrier of teachers quite easily and began yanking wigs off heads. Gasps of surprise came from the students. Gasps of horror came from the crowds of people who had flocked around to watch this new spectacle unfold.

Each and every student looked around them as though a spell had been broken. They were touching their bare heads, talking to each other.

"They have no hair," shouted a woman from the crowd, as though no one else could see what she was seeing.

"They look like convicts," another screamed.

Before Erin knew what was happening, the crowds were calling for Trefoil and Pro-Di-To to explain themselves. Simultaneously, out of the crowds hundreds of teenagers erupted, rushing towards the Trefoil children. Erin's heart thumped so hard she thought it would fly out of her chest. Something she had imagined ever since she knew about the four schools was happening before her very eyes.

The twins. The Teardrops had found them all, every one of the twins left behind at birth; those that were still alive. Some, sadly, had been told of the death of their twin yet they were still here to honour their memory.

The sea of blue became a storm at sea with twins finding each other, each one knowing precisely where their opposite was. Arms were thrown up and around, shouts of joy flew up like spray until the storm flattened out to a tranquil pool.

The police officers who had spread around the park not knowing what to make of all of this were immobile. Then a clap of hands and another then another until all the crowd and police clapped and cheered.

Tears of joy slid down her cheeks as she stood soaking all of this up. Then she was being shaken by someone. Miranda had grasped her shoulders. "Erin, look! They're escaping."

Erin stared and could just make out the three in white disappearing towards the road. She yelled for someone to stop them, but her one voice couldn't be heard over the thunderous chanting for Trefoil to be punished.

Miranda grabbed Erin's hand and pulled her away along the twisting paths towards the open road. Pushing through the torrents of people was like wading through water slowing their progress at every turn. Finally, they reached the road.

The coaches for the students were nowhere to be seen, just a steady stream of taxis and cars making their way along the road, meandering round the bend, all completely unaware of the momentous happenings that were unfolding just a few metres away.

Erin searched the faces around them, looking for someone she recognised. A sudden shout brought her vision quickly to Frankie and Cara, and she and Miranda sprinted to them through a sudden opening of the waves of people.

Joyce Williams and John Johnson were being held by several police officers, both of them writhing to escape from their captors. Frankie and Cara looked triumphant as Erin threw questions at them. "How? Where? When?"

"We did it!" shouted Frankie. "We got them."

"Where's Oliver Irons?" Erin yelled back.

Frankie's face clouded over, his smile vanishing like a light going out. "He's gone. He escaped in a car with Angela De Vate. Just now. We were too late."

By this time, Erin and Miranda had reached the tableau of police handcuffing the two members of Trefoil. Erin's chest heaved from the exertion of the chase. Miranda next to her was breathless. The two of them clung to each other. So near and yet so far, thought Erin.

"He won't get far, miss," said a police constable coming over to them. "We have the registration of the car, and we will do everything we can to capture him." The woman smiled at them. "You need to come with us. You all have a lot to explain. What a story. I can't wait to hear your side of it all."

Erin and Miranda, Frankie and Cara were led to police cars parked near the pavement. Before dipping her head to get into the car, Erin looked back at the park where hundreds of sets of twins and their parents were finally together. Each family hugging and talking, smiling and laughing. We did this, she thought. We set our butterflies free, and they have found their homes.

In the car, she looked at her twin. There was no need for words. They both knew.

Meg Tilstone <ceo@central_airport.com>

Pro-Di-To Lear Jet Police Investigation

To   Airport Board of Directors

A private Lear jet owned by Pro-Di-To took off from Gatwick at 18:00 hours. It is believed that the only two passengers were Oliver Irons and Angela De Vate. The police are questioning our ground crew to discover who helped their escape.

Traffic control monitored the flight which took them to Palermo Airport in Sicily.

On arrival, the Sicilian authorities boarded the plane. However, on completing a thorough search of the privately owned jet no one was discovered apart from the two pilots and four members of aircrew. They are currently being held and questioned.

Meg Tilstone

CEO Central Airport

Chapter 15

Two months later.

Miranda wrapped her scarf tighter and pulled her woolly hat down over her ears to keep any draughts out. It was freezing at The Seven Spirits. The sky, a washed-out grey, and a weak sun struggled to bring brightness to the December day. Beside her walked Frankie deep in thought. So much has happened since we were in Zephyr, she thought. Since we left too.

Also, making their way through the rough grass to the seven stones were their friends. Miranda said hi to each one in turn. So many friends. In Zephyr, friendship was forbidden, and yet you cannot fully control the heart. She had found Franklyn Mallory, and he had found her. She glanced across to him now as he laid a thick blanket on the grass. His flame-coloured hair reflected that of the small fire burning in the centre of the circle. He looked up as though sensing her appraisal and grinned. He performed a mock bow, and she sat down on the blanket.

Rob and Nadir had carried up a metal fire pit from Petra's house earlier in the day, and the logs within it were glowing white and crimson, the flames crackling amber and violet sparks. It was a live thing, needing oxygen, all-consuming and yet could be beaten back. Fight fire with fire, Miranda thought, remembering the two boats in the Thames. Just before she had run from the bridge, she had watched the two boats turn towards each other and a rocket shooting from one, hitting the other, causing an explosion. As fire engulfed *Bateau de Papier*, the wind blew sparks at *Papillon*. The last thing she had heard as she ran to the steps was the second boat blowing up. They had certainly ignited the truth but at what cost. The paper boat and the butterfly were no more.

She shivered. Frankie put his arm around her. "Cold?"

"A little," she said. She didn't want to tell him the truth.

Tea lights in glass jam jars set around the Spirits flickered in the night air. Shadows danced against the stones, just like those long-lost years ago. Miranda felt their presence tonight and even more so after she had walked their tunnel. The entrance by one of the Spirit rocks was protected now by ugly fencing until the Newton town council could decide what to do with it. There had been talk of opening it up for visitors. Miranda hoped that wouldn't happen, this was a special place.

The last few weeks had been exhausting. Answering the authorities' hundreds of questions and answering them repeatedly until they were finally satisfied. They had watched Joyce Williams and John Johnson's trial on a television set up in one of the rooms at court. Miranda had been astonished when Johnson had climbed up onto the barrier and managed to throw himself down the steep stairs to the cells below. Unlike Guy Fawkes all those years ago, he didn't kill himself. He fractured his leg in three places and broke his nose. Not quite the glorious end he had planned.

Oliver Irons along with Angela de Vate were still out there somewhere. The police had followed them to Sicily, and then the trail stopped. They had vanished. Miranda hoped they would find them before they carried on their desperate journey to power.

Someone thrust a mug of hot mulled wine at her, and looking up, she was pleased to see it was Cassie, Petra's sister. They had so much to catch up on, but tonight was not the night. Warm, glowing faces surrounded the flames. Laughing and joking, celebrating their night together just a few days before Christmas. Tonight, was a time to look forwards, not back, a time to have fun to toast their future.

Through the flames, she could see her twin sister snuggled up next to Nadir. He had his arm around her and whispering something, which caused Erin to cackle with laughter. What a glorious sound thought Miranda. And then an invisible line between the two girls pulled them together, and Erin looked up. She held up her mug, and Erin followed suit.

 I love you Miranda, Erin said inside her head. "Cheers," she whispered.

"What was that?" Nadir asked.

"Just talking to my sister," Erin said.

"How can she hear you from over here?"

"Oh, she knows what I'm thinking. Sometimes before I do."

They both fell silent. Comfortable just being together at last. Erin smiled to herself, remembering their first kiss.

It was back in early November, when they had come home from London, after all the interrogations. Erin had taken herself off to the coffee shop in Newton where Miranda had met with the Marstons all those months ago. While Erin sipped her latte, she scrolled through the photos Sergeant Marston had sent of the whole family together, with Daisy finally joining her twin.

Erin loved this café particularly because it wasn't huge, it was cosy. It wasn't flash and expensive. It was friendly and even better made great coffee. She had been savouring her drink when Nadir had appeared next to her table.

"Is this seat taken?" he asked.

"Yes, I mean no. No, it's not." Heat rose in her cheeks as she looked at her friend.

They had talked for hours until the people in the café told them it was closing time. When they had left, Nadir had taken her hand gently in his. He had stroked her face and then kissed her.

Now, in the chilly air of December, she leaned over to kiss him. He enfolded her in a hug that felt like home.

"Hey everyone," shouted Rob. Erin pulled away and looked over to where Rob was sitting with Willow. "I think we should have a toast."

"Great idea. I'm starving," replied Nadir. Groans erupted from all the others.

"Your jokes don't get any better, do they mate?" Rob said.

The banter flew around the circle for a few minutes before Rob stood up and, holding his mug aloft, shouted, "To freedom!"

Everyone responded the same and glugged back the warm wine.

"This is awful stuff," Rob said. "Where's the beer?"

The chatter and drinking went on into the night. Erin thought about her family. Mal was coming home soon from university for the holidays. Cara had asked him if they could be together, but he wasn't convinced. He had already met another girl in York, he told her. Secretly, Erin was pleased. Cara turned out all right in the end, but she still didn't like her.

Mum and Dad were pleased it was all over for the time being. Next year, the real court trials would begin once all the evidence had been collated. It was going to be a traumatic ordeal for everyone concerned. There was still so much to do, and tonight she said to herself, I am going to be a normal sixteen-year-old having fun with my friends.

A tiny kiss caressed her cheek and then another and another. Minute flakes of snow floated down, and suddenly the air was full of raucous singing, "I'm dreaming of a white Christmas."

She joined in, the well-known words coming to her easily. Erin laughed as her twin sister and her good friend, Frankie, tried to sing along too.

They didn't know the words, and it didn't matter.

Nothing mattered except love, family and friendship.

AUTHOR'S NOTE

My inspiration for the Paper Boats & Butterflies trilogy came during a memorable holiday in Fife, Scotland. On visiting a decommissioned underground nuclear bunker hidden below a farm, I wondered what else is under the ground that we don't know about. At around the same time, I wondered about families and how desperate someone would be to 'sell' their child. I brought these ideas together to create my stories.

As I wrote the three books, I found the following publications extremely helpful in understanding the human mind: *Nature via Nurture* (Matt Ridley) and *The Human Mind: and how to make the most of it* (Robert Winston). However, the events and characters are from my imagination. Some of the places mentioned are real, and others are fictional.

ACKNOWLEDGEMENTS

I knew from the start this story would be a trilogy. Erin and Miranda have taken me along a path of such twists and turns - some delightful, some painful - yet I have loved every minute and hope you have too. Creating the many characters, plots and settings has been an absolute joy, and I can now call myself a writer.

There are so many people to thank. My wonderful family who mean the world to me – thank you for loving and supporting me and for putting up with me. I love you all so much.

Thank you, once again, to Lauren Zorkoczy for creating a third gorgeous book cover. You have such talent!

Thank you to Becky Stewart for your fabulous illustrations that bring life to my books.

Thank you to the fantastic people who have proofread book 3 – Hannah Gold, Carolyn Moore, Emma Deards, Kaatje Evans. Your comments help so much in the drafting process.

Huge thanks must go to Annalie Maher and Deb Griffiths. Without them, these books would never have been written, and my self-belief would still be hiding under a rock on a beach somewhere! These two ladies have such amazing skills and knowledge between them, and I am proud to call them my friends. I just hope you will continue with me and my writing journey. I promise lots of lattes and fun on the way!

My final thanks go to my long-suffering husband, Chris. You are my heart and soul. I love you more than anything.

ABOUT THE AUTHOR

Sue lives in Buckinghamshire with her family and Kizzie, a mad flat-coated retriever.

Igniting the Truth is the third book of the PAPER BOATS & BUTTERFLIES trilogy.

Book 1, *Unfolding The Truth* and Book 2, *True Tears*, are available from all good bookshops and Amazon. For school bulk orders please visit Sue's website, **www.sueupton-author.com**

To discuss or book school author visits and to order the Scheme of Work for Key Stage 3, please email Sue, **info@sueupton-author.com**

You can also follow Sue on Instagram **@sue.upton_author**

Published by Budding Authors Assistant

www.help2publish.co.uk

Printed in Great Britain
by Amazon

Paper Boats & Butterflies Trilogy

Unfolding the Truth… (Book 1)

True Tears (Book 2)

Igniting the Truth… (Book 3)

Sue Upton
info@sueupton-author.com
First Published: September 2021
by
Budding Authors Assistant
www.help2publish.co.uk
Illustrations by Becky Stewart
Cover design by Lauren Zorkoczy

ISBN: 9781919625423

PAPER BOATS & BUTTERFLIES

Igniting the Truth...

Sue Upton

Illustrations by Becky Stewart

To Mum and Dad, Margaret and John,
with all my love and thanks.